哈福

第一本文法會話自學書

世界最強 英文文法會話

Speak Beautiful English in 30 Days

蘇盈盈—著

附 MP3

哈福

一次學好文法 & 會話

▶ 本書 5 大特色

- 幫助讀者突破文法盲點，協助老師「文法教學」更活潑
- 採用簡單又實用的動詞，以及平易近人的英語會話內容
- 帶著大家輕鬆突破「動詞變化」的文法瓶頸
- 能夠掌握「動詞變化」的人，要把英語學好就不難了
- 老師教學「不流汗」，學生聽課「不皺眉」，考試一樣拿高分，開口很流利

本書除了幫助讀者突破個人的文法盲點，亦能協助英語教師從事更活潑的「文法教學」。

很多人的英語學習經驗是痛苦的。台灣的英語教學為了應付升學考試，國高中課堂裡的「文法教學」就佔了百分之八十，也難怪思想活潑的學子會被「死氣沈沈」的英文課打敗。

▶ 簡易會話 靈活文法

說英語與說中文的最大相異之處，就是「動詞的時態變化」。其實我們所說的話，幾乎都存在著「時間」的影子。

中文的好處之一，就是不論過去、現在、還是未來，動詞的說法與寫法是不會變的。無論你是「正在」吃飯，還是「吃過」飯了，吃飯的「吃」都是同一個字，不會變成「吃 ing」也不會變成「吃 ed」。

　　說英語以及寫英文的時候，動詞則必須跟著時間觀念走。很多人在寫英文時，常犯的文法錯誤就是「動詞的時態變化」，更遑論在開口說英語時，嘴巴能夠自動把動詞變化「說清楚、講明白」。

▶ 不流汗 不皺眉 拿滿分

　　為了讓讀者輕鬆領會英文裡的「動詞變化」，我們以循序漸進，深入淺出的編排方式，採用簡單又實用的動詞，以及平易近人的英語會話內容，帶著大家從最易懂的「現在進行式」，一直到最令人困惑的「現在完成式」。

　　只要您能夠跟著每個單元的腳步走，再輔以專業美語老師所錄製的 MP3 邊聽邊學，一定能夠在短短的時間之內，輕鬆突破「動詞變化」的文法瓶頸。

　　簡而言之，能夠掌握「動詞變化」的人，要把英語學好就不難了。如果教「動詞變化」像是在說故事，聊生活，那麼老師也能教學「不流汗」，學生聽課「不皺眉」，考試一樣拿高分，開口一樣很流利。

作者　謹識

目錄

Chapter 2　現在簡單式

Chapter 3　未來式

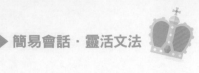

Chapter 4 will 和 shall 的用法

Chapter 5　過去式

Chapter 6 過去進行式

Chapter 7 現在完成式

Chapter 8　Used to

Chapter 9　助動詞

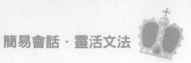

簡易會話・靈活文法

CHAPTER 1

現在進行式

我為什麼從現在進行式教起，而不是從現在簡單式教起，因為，現在簡單式是用的最少的一種動詞形式，我們說話的時候，最常用的是「現在」在做什麼，「過去」在做什麼，或是我「將」做什麼。現在簡單式反而較少用。

A 現在進行式最常見的用法就是，說某人現在正在做什麼事。

例如：客聽裡的電視聲音很大，但你正在房裡讀書，你就可以跟別人說：I'm studying.（我現在正在讀書），好讓他們把音量關小聲一點。

媽媽問瑪麗在哪裡，你回答說：她現在「正在」洗澡。英語就是：She is taking a bath. 。

B 現在進行式說的，不一定是說話的時候正在做的事情。

例如：你想知道對方在哪裡高就？你問他 Where are you working? 這個句子是用現在進行式，但是你跟他說話的時候，對方可能是在家裡，或是在宴會上，並不是正在上班，所以，你是問他「目前在哪裡高就」，而不是問對方「正在哪裡工作」。

C 我們如果提到情況的改變，也用現在進行式。

例如：

The cost of living is increasing.

生活費用真是越來越高。

These days food is becoming more expensive.

最近食物變得愈來愈貴了。

The world is changing.

世界在變。

Your daughter is becoming quite a young lady.

你的女兒徹底變成一個小姐了。

Is your math getting better?

你的數學有比較好了嗎？

以上這些句子都是說明「漸次在改變」的情況。

D 現在進行式除了表示，某人「現在正在做什麼」之外，也可以說，某件事「現在沒有在進行」，也就是文法上說的「現在進行式的否定句」。

例如，原本外頭一直在下雨，後來雨停了，於是想出門去玩的你，就很開心的說：

It's not raining now.

（現在沒有在下雨了。）

E 現在簡單式也可以用在疑問句，問對方現在的情形。

例如：你在宴會上遇到瑪麗，你問她：「宴會上玩得愉快嗎？」宴會還沒有結束，瑪麗是否玩得愉快，要用現在進行式來問，Are you enjoying the party?

F 我們也用進行式來表達，「最近這一段時間在做的事」，說話的當時，你可能並沒有正在做這件事，但是，最近一直都有在做這件事。

例如：

What are you doing these days?

你最近在做什麼？

You are working hard today.

你今天很努力工作。

John isn't playing football this season.

約翰這一個球季不打足球。

UNIT 01 | I'm trying…

我正想要…

Dialogue 1

A : Could you please be quiet?
I'm trying to concentrate.

可以請你安靜一點嗎？
我正想要專心。

B : I'm sorry, I didn't realize you were studying.

對不起，我不知道你正在唸書。

A : That's all right. Just keep it down.

沒關係，只要放低音量。

B : Hey, no problem.

嘿，沒問題。

心靈雞湯

try 是試試看的意思，但在英語口語中，I am trying to…指的是「我正想要去做某件事」，而非「我正試著要去做某件事」。

Dialogue 2

A : Henry, could you turn the TV down?
I'm trying to sleep.

亨利，你可以把電視關掉嗎？
我正想要睡覺。

B : Sure thing.
I'm sorry if I woke you up.

當然。抱歉把你吵醒了。

A : That's all right.
I'll see you in the morning.

沒關係。明早見。

B : Good night John.

晚安，約翰。

單字

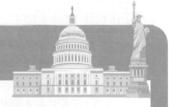

quiet	[ˈkwaɪət]	形 安靜的
concentrate	[ˈkɑnsɛnˌtret]	動 專心；專注於
realize	[ˈriəˌlaɪz]	動 明瞭；知道
problem	[ˈprɑbləm]	名 問題

UNIT 02 | Mary is taking a shower.

瑪麗正在洗澡

Dialogue 1

A : Mary is taking a shower.
You could wait in the living room for her.
瑪麗正在淋浴。
你可以在客廳等她。

B : Okay.
Is it all right if I use your phone?
好的。我可以借用你的電話嗎？

A : Sure, it's on the table there.
I'll tell Mary to hurry.
當然，它在那邊桌上。
我去叫瑪麗快一點。

B : Don't do that; there's no rush.
別這麼做，我不趕時間。

Dialogue 2

A : Janis is taking a cab to the hotel.
珍妮絲正搭計程車前往飯店。

B ： Her plane landed on time then I guess.

那我猜她搭的班機有準時降落。

A ： Actually it was early.

She said she would meet us at the hotel.

事實上班機提早了。

她說她會在飯店和我們見面。

B ： Well, let's get going.

嗯，我們走吧。

單字

shower	[ʃaʊr]	名 淋浴
living room		名 起居室
hurry	[ˈhɝɪ]	動 匆忙；趕快
rush	[rʌʃ]	名 緊急的；急著趕
cab	[kæb]	名 計程車
land	[lænd]	動 著陸
actually	[ˈæktʃʊəlɪ]	副 實際上；事實上
early	[ˈɝlɪ]	副 早

UNIT 03 | Where are you working?

你在哪裡高就？

Dialogue 1

A : Where are you working now?

你現在哪裡高就？

B : I'm working with Children's Services.

我在做兒童服務工作。

A : No kidding, how do you like it?

真的，你喜歡嗎？

B : It's a tough job, but I feel like I'm doing something important.

這是份困難的工作，但是我感覺我在做某些重要的事情。

Dialogue 2

A : I am working on a project with Will.

我現在和威爾在一起做一個企劃。

B ： Oh how exciting!
He is so great at what he does.

噢，真令人興奮！

他做的每件事情都很成功。

A ： I know, I have learned so much just from working with him.

我知道，和他工作後我已經學到很多了。

B ： Let me know how your project works out.

讓我知道你們的企劃結果如何。

單字

tough	[tʌf]	形 （口語）艱難
important	[ɪmˈpɔrtənt]	形 重要的
project	[ˈprɑdʒɛkt]	名 專案；企畫
exciting	[ɪkˈsaɪtɪŋ]	形 令人興奮的
learn	[lɝn]	動 學習

MP3-5

UNIT 04

These days food is becoming more expensive.

最近食物變得愈來愈貴了。

Dialogue 1

A : These days food is becoming more expensive.

最近食物變得愈來愈貴了。

B : I know what you mean.
Even my grocery bills are high.

我知道你在說什麼。

甚至我的雜貨帳單都變貴了。

A : Well, when you're feeding three children, I suppose that's normal.

嗯，當你有三個孩子要養，我想這是正常的。

B : Yes, I suppose it is.

沒錯，我想也是。

Dialogue 2

A : Your daughter is becoming quite a young lady.

你的女兒徹底變成一個小姐了。

B ： Yes, she is.
It seems like yesterday she was a baby.

是啊，她是。
好像昨天的她還是個嬰兒。

A ： Children do grow up fast.

孩子長大的很快。

B ： Too fast if you ask me.

如果你問我，我會說太快了。

單字

expensive	[ɪkˈspɛnsɪv]	形 昂貴的
mean	[min]	動 意思是
grocery	[ˈgrosərɪ]	名 雜貨
bill	[bɪl]	名 帳單
feed	[fid]	動 餵食
suppose	[səˈpoz]	動 認為理應的
normal	[ˈnɔrml]	形 一般的；正常的

UNIT 05 | The world is changing.

MP3-6

世界在變。

Dialogue 1

A : The world is changing.

世界在變了。

B : You're right there.
The world was different only ten years ago.

你說的對。

十年前的世界跟現在都不一樣了。

A : Technology has revolutionized how we live.
It's just amazing to me.

科技把我們的生活方式來了個大改革。

對我來說真的很不可思議。

B : It is amazing.
Just imagine what the next century will bring.

太不可思議了。

想想看下個世紀會變得怎麼樣。

Dialogue 2

A : Is your math getting better?

你的數學有比較好了嗎？

B ： Actually yes, I got an A on my last test.

事實上是的，我上次考試得了一個 A。

A ： That's great. I guess that tutor really helped.

太好了。我想那個家教真的有幫助。

B ： Oh yes, she helped a lot.

噢，是的，她幫了很大的忙。

單字

world	[wɔld]	名 世界
right	[raɪt]	形 正確
different	[ˈdɪfərənt]	形 不同的
technology	[tɛkˈnɑlədʒɪ]	名 科技
revolutionize	[ˌrɛvəˈluʃənˌaɪz]	動 革命性巨變
amazing	[əˈmezɪŋ]	形 令人驚嘆的
imagine	[ɪˈmædʒɪn]	動 想像
century	[ˈsɛntʃərɪ]	名 世紀
tutor	[ˈtjutɚ]	名 家庭教師

UNIT 06 | It isn't raining now.

MP3-7

沒有在下雨了。

Dialogue 1

A : It isn't raining now.
   沒有在下雨了。

B : Well, look at that.
   I thought it would never stop.
   嗯，你看看。
   我以為它永遠不會停了呢。

A : Do you want to drive to the park now?
   你現在想要開車去公園嗎？

B : Yes, the sun is coming back again.
   好啊！太陽又出來回來了。

Dialogue 2

A : Can you believe it isn't raining?
   你會相信現在沒有下雨了嗎？

B : No, I can't.
I don't know what to do now that there's sunshine.

不，我真不敢相信。

出太陽了，但，我不知道要做什麼。

A : Why don't we just take a walk and enjoy it?

我們何不散個步享受一下？

B : Good idea, let me get my jacket.

好主意，讓我去拿我的夾克。

單字

thought	[θɔt]	動 想（think 的過去式）；認為
drive	[draɪv]	動 開車
believe	[bɪˈliv]	動 相信
sunshine	[ˈsʌnˌʃaɪn]	名 陽光
enjoy	[ɪnˈdʒɔɪ]	動 享受；感到樂趣
jacket	[ˈdʒækɪt]	名 夾克；外套

UNIT 07 | Are you enjoying the party?

MP3-8

妳喜歡這個派對嗎？

Dialogue 1

A : Hello Mary, are you enjoying the party?

哈囉，瑪麗，妳喜歡這個派對嗎？

B : Yes, I am. Thank you.
The band is great.

是的，謝謝。樂團很棒。

A : Aren't they?
That's my brother's band.

難道不是嗎？那是我哥哥的樂團。

B : You're kidding!
I didn't even know he played.

你在開玩笑！我根本不知道他會演奏。

Dialogue 2

A : Are you enjoying the veal, Mrs. Cane?

肯恩太太，妳喜歡小牛肉嗎？

B ： Very much.

My compliments to your chef.

很喜歡。

代我向你的廚師致意。

A ： I'm sure he sends his thanks.

Can I get you anything?

我確定他會向妳道謝。

你還要吃些什麼嗎？

B ： I'd love to try that delicious looking cheesecake.

我想要吃吃看那些看起來很美味的起司蛋糕。

單字

band	[bænd]	名 樂團
veal	[vil]	名 小牛肉
compliment	[ˈkɑmpləmənt]	名 誇獎；讚美
chef	[ʃɛf]	名 廚師
delicious	[dɪˈlɪʃəs]	形 好吃的；美味的

UNIT 08 | What are you doing these days?

你近來在做什麼？

Dialogue 1

A : What are you doing these days?

你近來在做什麼？

B : I'm going to school now.

我現在在上學。

A : Good for you!
Are you going full-time or taking night classes?

有你的！你是全職上課，還是上夜校？

B : Full-time...I want to get my master's in geology.

我是全職上課，我想要唸一個地質學碩士。

Dialogue 2

A : John isn't playing football this season.

約翰這一個球季沒有踢足球。

B ： Why not? I thought he loved the sport.

為什麼沒有？我以為他喜愛這個那運動。

A ： Oh he does, but the doctor said that if he wanted his knee to heal properly, he'd have to take a season off.

哦，他是喜歡，但是醫師說如果他想要讓他的膝蓋徹底痊癒，他必需休息一個球季。

B ： Well, I guess that's for the better then.

嗯，我想那樣比較好。

單字

geology	[dʒɪˈalədʒɪ]	名 地質學
football	[ˈfʊtˌbɔl]	名 美式足球
season	[ˈsizn̩]	名 一個球季
sport	[spɔrt]	名 運動
knee	[ni]	名 膝蓋
heal	[hil]	動 治癒
properly	[ˈprapɚlɪ]	副 適當地

UNIT 09 | You're working hard today. 你今天工作很認真。

MP3-10

Dialogue 1

A : You're working hard today.
你今天工作很認真。

B : I have to finish this report by 5:00.
我必須在 **5:00** 以前完成這份報告。

A : Do you need any help with anything?
你有任何事情需要幫忙嗎？

B : Yeah, if you could proofread what I already have, that would really help.
有，如果你能幫我校對我已經寫好的部份，那真的是幫了大忙。

Dialogue 2

A : What are you working on?
你在做什麼？

B： I'm designing the main hall of the museum.

我正在設計博物館的大廳。

A： Do you think you could take the left wing also?

你認為你也可以做左側廳的部份嗎？

B： Yes, if I could get an assistant to help.

可以，如果我可以有一位助手幫忙的話。

單字

finish	[ˈfɪnɪʃ]	動 完成
report	[rɪˈport]	名 報告
proofread	[ˈprufˈrid]	動 校對
already	[ɔlˈrɛdɪ]	副 已經
design	[dɪˈzaɪn]	動 設計
hall	[hɔl]	名 大廳
museum	[mjuˈzɪəm]	名 博物館
main	[men]	形 主要的
wing	[wɪŋ]	名 建築的側廳
assistant	[əˈsɪstənt]	名 助手

心靈雞湯

Never eat a sugared doughnut when wearing a dark suit.
當你穿深色衣服時，千萬別吃灑滿糖粉的甜甜圈。

美國風情文化

在紐約街頭，常有許多販賣甜甜圈的早餐車，這些早餐車還會賣咖啡。

一份甜甜圈大概是一點五美金或是兩塊美金，而一杯咖啡的價錢為七十五分美金或是一塊錢美金。

美國風情文化

甜甜圈的口味通常有肉桂以及巧克力兩種，donut 上面都會灑上厚厚的糖粉和肉桂粉，有些 donut 裡頭還會夾著糖漿。

CHAPTER 2

現在簡單式

我們學動詞的時式，學到現在簡單式的時候，常常因為「現在」兩個字，而以為現在在做的事情就是要用現在簡單式，其實現在簡單式，是與「時間」無關的事情。因為，如果是現在在做的動作，那就要用現在進行式，如果提到過去的事情，就要用過去式，將來的事情則要用未來式。

A 我們用「現在簡單式」來說明一件事實，例如：

約翰是一位公車司機，所以我們說：

John drives a bus.（約翰開公車。）這是一件事實，但是如果我們要說約翰現在正在開公車，英語就應該是：

John is driving a bus.

但是約翰也可能現在不在開公車，而是在睡覺，我們就說：

John is not driving a bus. He is asleep.

但是，這並不能改變 John drives a bus.（約翰是開公車的。）這個事實。

B 如果我們說，在台灣大多數商店都開到晚上十點，這也是在陳述一件事實，英語也同樣要用現在簡單式。

例如：

In Taiwan, most stores close at 10:00 p.m.

C 另一個要用現在簡單式的事實，就是大自然的狀況，例如：

The earth goes around the sun.（地球繞著太陽運轉。）
The sun rises in the east.（太陽從東方升起。）

D 一個人平常的習慣，或是他一般都這麼做的事，也是要用現在簡單式：

I go to work by bus.（我搭公車上班。）
I go through a travel agency to plan my vacations.
（我都是透過旅行社來安排我的假期。）

E　當我們提到有時間表的，例如：火車幾點開，或是安排好的活動，例如：電影幾點上映，球賽幾點開始等等也是要用「現在簡單式」：

The football game starts at 2:00.
（足球比賽兩點開始。）

What time does the concert begin?
（音樂會幾點開始？）

What time does the movie begin?
（電影幾點開始？）

The train leaves Taipei at 6:30 a.m. and arrives in Taiwan at noon.
（火車早上六點半離開台北，中午抵達台南。）

F　注意：我們問對方「從哪裡來的」要用現在簡單式，因為這也是個人的一件事實狀況：

Where do you come from?
（你從哪裡來？）

He comes from Japan.
（他從日本來。）

G　問對方「多常 (how often)」做一件事，也是要用現在簡單式：

How often do you go to the dentist?
（你多久去看一次牙醫？）

How often do you go to the mall?
（你多久去一次購物中心？）

UNIT 10 Most donut shops open at 7：00 a.m.

MP3-11

大部分的甜甜圈商店在早上七點開門。

Dialogue 1

A : Most donut shops open at 7:00 a.m.

大部分的甜甜圈商店在早上七點開門。

B : Great. If I can get there right at 7:00, I'll have plenty of time to get to work.

很好。如果我可以在七點整到那裡，我就會有充足的時間去上班。

A : Could you pick up some bagels for me?

你可以幫我帶一些貝果麵包嗎？

B : Sure, just write down what you want, and I'll get it while I'm there.

當然，寫下你想要什麼，我去那裡時會買。

Dialogue 2

A : Most banks aren't open on Sunday.

大多數的銀行星期天都不開門。

B： I guess I'll just have to wait until Monday to cash my check.

　　我想我只能等到星期一再兌現我的支票了。

A： I believe the bank down the road opens Monday morning at 9:00.

　　我相信路底的那家銀行星期一早上九點開門。

B： Okay, I'll be there right at 9:00 then.

　　好的，九點整我會到那裏。

單字

donut	[ˈdonət]	名 甜甜圈
shop	[ʃɑp]	名 小店
plenty	[ˈplɛntɪ]	形 很多
bagel	[ˈbeɡḷ]	名 貝果麵包
bank	[bæŋk]	名 銀行
guess	[ɡɛs]	動 猜想
cash	[kæʃ]	動 兌現
check	[tʃɛk]	名 支票

MP3-12

UNIT 11 | I go to work by bus.

我搭公車上班。

Dialogue 1

A : I go to work by bus.

我搭公車上班。

B : Don't you miss driving a car?

你不懷念開車上班的日子嗎？

A : Not really. On the bus I can look over my work on the way there.

不會耶。搭公車，我可以在路上把我的工作看一遍。

B : I see.
Maybe I'll try taking the bus next week.

原來如此。
也許下個禮拜我也試著搭公車。

Dialogue 2

A : I go through a travel agency to plan my vacations.

我都是透過旅行社來安排我的假期。

B : That's probably the best way, especially if the travel agent is good.

那可能是最好的方式，特別是旅行社很好的時候。

A : Mary is good.

I've enjoyed every vacation she has set up for me.

瑪麗很好。

她為我安排的每一次假期我都很喜歡。

B : Would you mind giving me her number?

I want to go on vacation next summer.

你介意給我她的聯絡電話嗎？

我明年夏天要去渡假。

生活小常識

wing 原來是指鳥類的翅膀，不過，飛機的「機翼」，或是建築物的「側廳」，亦可稱做 wing。
當你在美國超是買東西時，看到包裝上寫著 wing 的，就是雞翅膀。

單字

miss	[mɪs]	動 想念
bus	[bʌs]	名 公車
through	[θru]	介 經由
travel	[ˈtrævl̩]	名 旅行
agency	[ˈedʒənsɪ]	名 代理商；辦事處
vacation	[vəˈkeʃən]	名 休假；假期
probably	[ˈprɑbəblɪ]	副 或許；可能的
especially	[əˈspɛʃəlɪ]	副 特別是
agent	[ˈedʒənt]	名 代理人

UNIT 12 I don't smoke.

MP3-13

我不抽煙。

Dialogue 1

A : Would you like a cigarette?
你要來一根煙嗎？

B : No thanks, I don't smoke.
不，謝謝。我不抽煙。

A : I've been trying to quit.
I'm just not feeling very good.
我一直試著在戒煙。
我現在感覺不是很好。

B : I'm sure quitting would make you feel better.
我確定戒了煙之後會讓你感覺更好。

Dialogue 2

A ： Could you give me a lift across town?
你可以載我到城的另一邊嗎？

B ： I would if I could, but I don't drive.
如果我可以我會載你，但是我不開車。

A ： Why on earth do you not drive?
究竟是為了什麼你不開車呢？

B ： I don't have a car. I ride the bus.
我沒有車，我搭公車。

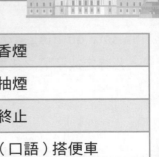

單字

cigarette	[sɪgəˈrɛt]	名 香煙
smoke	[smok]	動 抽煙
Quit	[kwɪt]	動 終止
lift	[lɪft]	名 （口語）搭便車
drive	[draɪv]	動 開車

UNIT 13 | Do you speak English?

MP3-14

你會說英文嗎？

Dialogue 1

A： Do you speak English?

你會說英文嗎？

B： Yes, ma'am I do.
Can I help you?

是的，我會。有什麼事嗎？

A： Yes, do you know when the parade will begin?

是的，你知道遊行什麼時候開始嗎？

B： 10:00, ma'am, I would pick out a spot now.

小姐，是十點，我會現在就挑一個好地點。

心靈雞湯

Surprise a new neighbor with one of your favorite homemade dishes.

宴請新鄰居一道你最喜愛的家鄉菜，讓他驚喜。

45

Dialogue 2

A : Do you understand English?

你懂英文嗎？

B : I understand a little English.
What do you need?

我懂一點英文。
你要什麼？

A : I'd like to try that beef dish, and drink a beer.

我想要試那一道牛肉，還要一杯啤酒。

B : Okay, I'll get it for you.

好的，我幫你拿。

單字

parade	[pəˈred]	名 遊行
spot	[spɑt]	名 位置；地點
understand	[ˌʌndɚˈstænd]	動 瞭解；明白
dish	[dɪʃ]	名 一碟菜

UNIT 14 | The football game starts at 2:00.

MP3-15

足球比賽兩點開始。

Dialogue 1

A : The football game starts at 2:00.
足球比賽兩點開始。

B : We'd better hurry then, it's already 1:30.
那我們最好趕快，現在已經是一點半了。

A : Do you have the tickets and some money?
你有票和錢嗎？

B : Yeah, I've got them right here. Let's go.
有，就在這裏。走吧。

Dialogue 2

A : What time does the concert begin?
音樂會幾點開始？

B : The concert starts at 7:00, but the reception is still going on now.
音樂會七點開始，但是歡迎會現在還在進行中。

A : I'm not concerned about the reception.

Let's just make the concert on time.

我不關心歡迎會。

我們準時抵達音樂會就可以。

B : No problem, we're at the concert hall now.

沒問題，我們現在正在音樂廳裏。

單字

football	[ˈfʊt,bɔl]	名 美式足球
game	[gem]	名 （球類）比賽
already	[ɔlˈrɛdɪ]	副 已經
hurry	[ˈhɝɪ]	動 匆忙；趕快
concert	[ˈkɑnsɚt]	名 演奏會；音樂會
reception	[rɪˈsɛpʃən]	名 招待會；歡迎會
concerned	[kənˈsɝnd]	形 關切；擔心的（concern 的過去分詞）
hall	[hɔl]	名 大廳

UNIT 15 | What time does the movie begin?

MP3-16

電影幾點開始？

Dialogue 1

A : What time does the movie begin?

電影幾點開始？

B : I think it starts at 6:30.
Do we have time to grab something to eat?

我想它 **6:30** 開始。
我們有時間去弄一些東西來吃嗎？

A : As long as it's fast food.

只要是速食就可以。

B : Hey, I love McDonald's.
Let's go for it.

嘿，我喜歡麥當勞，
我們去買吧。

Dialogue 2

A : What time does the game begin?

比賽幾點開始？

B : Don't worry. We've got plenty of time.
The game starts at 1:00.

別擔心。我們還有很多時間。
比賽一點開始。

A : Shouldn't we be there early?

我們不應該早點到那裏嗎？

B : It's only 11:00. Stop worrying.
We won't miss the game.

現在才 **11:00**，別擔心。
我們不會錯過比賽的。

單字

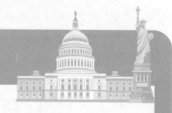

grab	[græb]	動 匆忙地拿
early	[ˈɝlɪ]	副 早
miss	[mɪs]	動 錯過
worry	[ˈwɝɪ]	動 憂慮；擔心

UNIT 16 | What do you do?

MP3-17

你的職業是什麼？

Dialogue 1

A : So what do you do?

那你的職業是什麼？

B : I'm a pediatrician.
I work at Doctors Hospital in the pediatric ward.

我是個小兒科醫師。
我在大夫醫院的小兒科病房上班。

A : Wow, it must be hard working with sick children.

哇，照顧生病的小孩一定是件辛苦的工作。

B : Some people feel that way, but children can be great patients.
I enjoy working with them.

有些人那麼想，但兒童是很好的病人。
我喜歡照顧他們。

Dialogue 2

A : I'm a CEO for Nortel.
What do you do?

我是北電的執行長。
你在從事什麼行業？

B : I'm a technical writer for one of your competitors - TI.

我是你其中一個競爭者－ **TI** 公司的技術作者。

A : Do you enjoy your work?

你喜歡你的工作嗎？

B : Absolutely!
I work from home, I set my own hours, and I love what I write about.

非常喜歡完全地！
我在家裏工作，自己安排時間，而且我喜愛我寫的東西。

心靈雞湯

Give your best to your employer.
把你最好的才能，貢獻給你的雇主。

單字

pediatrician	[ˌpidɪəˈtrɪʃən]	名 小兒科醫生
pediatric	[ˌpidɪˈætrɪk]	形 小兒科的
ward	[wɔrd]	名 病房
sick	[sɪk]	形 生病；不舒服
patient	[ˈpeʃənt]	形 有耐心的； 名 病人
competitor	[kəmˈpɛtɪtɚ]	名 競爭對手
technical	[ˈtɛknɪkəl]	形 技術上的
absolutely	[ˈæbsəˌlutlɪ]	副 絕對

心靈雞湯

Don't discuss salaries.
請勿討論薪水。

UNIT 17 | Where do you come from?

你從哪裡來？

Dialogue 1

A : Where do you come from?
你從哪裏來？

B : I'm from South Africa.
I'm on a business trip to Washington.
我從南非來。
我要到華盛頓洽公。

A : How interesting!
Are you enjoying America?
那多有趣！
你喜歡美國嗎？

B : Oh yes of course, but I do miss my home.
哦，那當然是的，但是我真的很想家。

Dialogue 2

A : Where did this letter come from?
這信從哪裏來的？

B : I don't know; there is no return address.

我不知道，沒有寄件人地址。

A : I wonder who sent it.

The stamp is a Chinese stamp.

我納悶是誰寄的。

郵票是張中國郵票。

B : Well, then it probably came from China.

嗯，那麼可能是從中國寄來的。

單字

business	[ˈbɪznɪs]	名 生意；商務
trip	[trɪp]	名 旅程；旅遊
interesting	[ˈɪntrɪstɪŋ]	形 有趣的
miss	[mɪs]	動 想念
return	[rɪˈtɝn]	動 回覆
wonder	[ˈwʌndɚ]	動 想；想知道
stamp	[stæmp]	名 郵票
probably	[ˈprɑbəblɪ]	副 或許；可能的

UNIT 18 How often do you go to the dentist?

你多久去看一次牙醫？

Dialogue 1

A : How often do you go to the dentist?
你多久去看一次牙醫？

B : I go twice a year for checkups.
我一年去兩次作檢查。

A : I guess your insurance covers those costs.
我猜你的保險支付那些費用。

B : Oh yes.
Since I go so routinely, I hardly ever need serious work on my teeth.
哦，是的。
因為我都按時去，我的牙齒幾乎不需要動什麼大工程。

Dialogue 2

A : How often do you go to the mall?

你多久去一次購物中心？

B : I only go at Christmastime really.
I'm not a mall person.

事實上我只有在聖誕節時會去。
我不是個愛去購物中心的人。

A : I'm not either but my friends just love malls.

我也不是，但是我的朋友都很愛購物中心。

B : Maybe you should suggest a different place to hang
out with your friends.

也許你應該建議一個不同的地方和你的朋友去走走。

Have regular medical and dental checkups.
定期做健康檢查與牙齒檢查。

單字

dentist	[ˈdɛntɪst]	名 牙醫
checkup	[ˈtʃɛkəp]	名 檢查
insurance	[ɪnˈʃʊrəns]	名 保險
cover	[ˈkʌvɚ]	動 包括
routinely	[ruˈtinlɪ]	副 定期的
hardly	[ˈhɑrdlɪ]	副 幾乎不
serious	[ˈsɪrɪəs]	形 嚴重的
teeth	[tiθ]	名 牙齒
often	[ˈɔfən]	副 時常
mall	[mɔl]	名 大型購物中心
suggest	[səˈdʒɛst]	動 建議

CHAPTER 3

未來式

未來式的用法,是英語的動詞時式裡,比較不會混淆的一個時式,因為只要是說到「將來」要做的事情,那就是要用「未來式」,只是未來式的說法有好幾種,這是讀者要特別注意的地方。

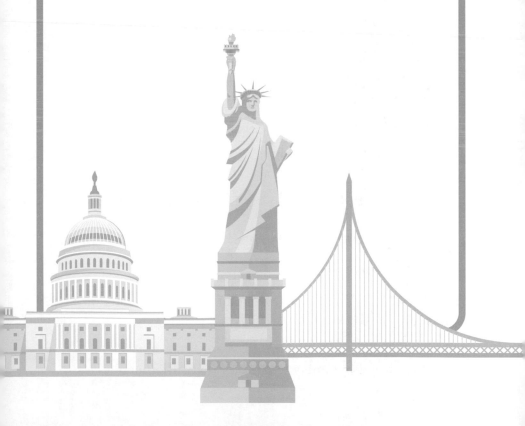

A 已經決定好將來某個時候要做的事，可以用「be 動詞＋現在分詞」來表達，我們以約翰下星期的行程來說：

He is going to the dentist on Monday.
（他星期一要去看牙醫。）

He is playing tennis on Friday afternoon.
（他星期五下午要打網球。）

He is going to the movies with Mary Saturday evening.
（他星期六晚上要跟瑪麗去看電影。）

B 如果是問對方有什麼預定的行程，那就要用「疑問句」來問。

例如：你問對方，這個週末要做什麼？
What are you doing this weekend?
　　或是你問對方，你打算作這件事嗎？例如：

Are you going shopping?
　　（你要去購物嗎？）
　　這句話是在問對方有沒有這個行程的計畫。

C 已經決定好將來要做的事，也可以用「be going to 原型動詞」的方式來表達。

　　例如：下面那一句話 John is playing tennis on Friday afternoon.（他星期五下午要打網球。）說明約翰計畫好星期五下午要去打網球，也可以說，
John is going to play tennis on Friday afternoon.

D 「be going to ＋原型動詞」的句型也可以用在，我們說出一件「我們認為會發生的事」，例如：你看滿天烏雲，你說，

It's going to rain.
（快要下雨了。）

又例如，大夥兒在機場等飛機，眼看著飛機起飛的時間就快到了，約翰還沒到，認為約翰會趕不上飛機，你就說：

John is going to miss his plane.
（約翰會趕不上飛機。）

E 如果你是說話的當兒決定要做什麼事，例如：大家在討論今晚要去哪裡，你考慮的結果，決定今晚留在家裡看書，這個決定並不是你事先計畫好的，而是現在才決定的，就要用 will 來表達：

I think I'll stay home tonight.
（我今晚想待在家裏。）

F will 也可以用在「提議」幫對方的忙時，例如：你看到對方拿了一個很重的袋子，你走過去跟他說，那個袋子看起來很重，我來幫你拿吧，I'll help you with the bag.

G will 也可以用在「同意」或「保證」對方你願意去做某件事。

　　例如：你需要用錢，正好手頭沒錢，你就跟朋友借，並跟他保證說，I'll pay you back tomorrow.（我明天會還你。）

H 你如果是要「答應」或「保證」你不會這麼做，那就要說 I won't…。

　　例如：朋友跟你說了一個秘密，要你答應不會說出去，你跟他保證你不會說出去，你就說 I won't tell anyone.（我不會告訴任何人。）

MEMO

UNIT 19 | We are having a party next Friday.

我們下週五要舉行一個宴會。

Dialogue 1

A : We are having a party next Friday.
Would you like to come?

　　我們下週五要舉行一個宴會。
　　你要來嗎？

B : Next Friday, yeah I think I'm free.
I'd love to come.

　　下週五，好啊。我想我有空。
　　我很高興能參加。

A : Great. It's a costume party so dress up.

　　太好了。這是場化妝舞會，所以好好打扮吧。

B : Cool, I love costume parties.

　　酷，我愛化妝舞會。

Dialogue 2

A : Hey, we're having a cookout this weekend.
Come over.

　　嗨，這個週末我們要在我家後院烤肉。
　　來參加吧。

B : I'm going out of town this weekend, otherwise I'd go.

　　我這個週末要出城去，不然我就會來。

A : Well, that stinks.
Why don't we have one when you get back?

　　啊！那太糟了。
　　我們何不等你回來以後再去野炊？

B : Sure, I'll give you a call.

　　好啊，我會打電話給你。

心靈雞湯

fun 指的是有趣的，好玩的，是屬於比較正面的形容詞。
而 funny 指的是可笑的，滑稽的，屬於較負面的形容詞。

單字

costume	[ˈkɑstjum]	名 服裝
cookout	[ˈkʊkaʊt]	名 （在自家後院的）露天烤肉
weekend	[ˈwikˈɛnd]	名 週末
otherwise	[ˈʌðɚˌwaɪz]	副 否則；不然
back	[bæk]	副 回來；名 背部

MEMO

MP3-21

UNIT 20

Mary is getting married next week.

瑪麗下週要結婚了。

Dialogue 1

A : Mary is getting married next week.

瑪麗下週要結婚了。

B : Is she really?
I didn't know that.

真的嗎？
我不知道這件事。

A : Well, I think she and her fiance are eloping.

嗯，我認為她和她的未婚夫是要私奔。

B : We can get them a gift anyway.

我們還是可以送他們一份禮物。

Dialogue 2

A : What's going on?

近來如何？

B : Susan is getting an award for her work.

蘇珊的工作表現得到了一份獎賞。

A : Wow, she must have impressed the boss.

哇，她一定讓老闆印象深刻。

B : I suppose so, he hands out awards every month for productivity and things like that.

我想是的，他每個月會為了生產力及類似的事頒發獎賞。

單字

really	[ˈrɪəlɪ]	副	真的
fiance	[fiˌɑnˈse]	名	未婚夫
elope	[ɪˈlop]	動	私奔
gift	[gɪft]	名	禮物
award	[əˈwɔrd]	名	獎賞
impress	[ɪmˈprɛs]	動	使印象深刻
boss	[bɔs]	名	主管；老闆

UNIT 21 | I'm working tomorrow morning.

明天早上我要上班。

Dialogue 1

A : What are you doing tomorrow morning?
你明天早上要做什麼？

B : I'm working tomorrow morning.
明天早上我要上班。

A : Okay, could we meet for lunch?
好的，我們可以碰面吃個午餐嗎？

B : I could do that.
Come by work at noon and we'll go out.
我可以。
中午來我的辦公室，我們可以出去。

Dialogue 2

A ： I can't go out tonight.
I'm studying for a test.

今晚我不能出門。
我要唸書準備考試。

B ： You have been studying all week.
Give yourself a break.

你已經唸了整個禮拜的書了。
休息一下吧。

A ： This is my last major grade for the semester.
Let me study tonight, and we'll go out tomorrow night.

這是我這學期最後一個主要的成績。
讓我今晚先唸書，然後我們明天晚上可以出去。

B ： All right.
Don't work too hard.

好的。
不要唸得太累了。

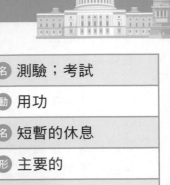

單字

test	[tɛst]	名 測驗；考試
study	[ˈstʌdɪ]	動 用功
break	[brek]	名 短暫的休息
major	[ˈmedʒɚ]	形 主要的
grade	[gred]	名 成績
semester	[səˈmɛstɚ]	名 學期
hard	[hɑrd]	副 努力的

心靈雞湯

Know how to tie a bow tie.
要知道如何打蝶型領結。

UNIT 22 | What are you doing this weekend?

MP3-23

你這個週末要做什麼？

A : What are you doing this weekend?
你這個週末要做什麼？

B : Oh, nothing special. Why?
哦，沒什麼特別的。為什麼這麼問？

A : I was wondering if you could help me move.
我在想你是否可以幫我搬家。

B : Sure. Let me know when to be at your house.
當然。告訴我什麼時候要到你家。

Dialogue 2

A : So what are you doing tonight?
你今晚要做什麼？

B ： Well, I've got to read for class and do some laundry.

嗯，我得為修的課念點書，還要準備上課還要洗衣服。

A ： That sounds fun.
Call me later.

聽起來滿好玩的。
稍後打電話給我。

B ： I will. Bye.

我會的。拜拜。

單字

special	[ˈspɛʃəl]	形 特別的
move	[muv]	動 搬家
laundry	[ˈlɔndrɪ]	名 待洗的衣物
sound	[saʊnd]	動 聽起來
fun	[fʌn]	形 好玩；樂趣

UNIT 23 | Are you going shopping?

你要去購物嗎？

Dialogue 1

A : Are you going shopping?
你要去購物嗎？

B : I'm going shopping for groceries.
我要去雜貨店採購。

A : Oh no, I thought you were going shopping for clothes.
哦不，我以為你是要去買衣服。

B : I plan on going clothes shopping next weekend.
我計畫下個週末去買衣服。

Dialogue 2

A : Are you going hiking this weekend?
你這個週末要去健行嗎？

B ： Yeah.

Do you want to go with me?

是的。

你要一起去嗎？

A ： Sure, why not?

I need the exercise.

好啊。

我需要運動。

B ： Okay. Well, I'll see you there.

好。到那邊見。

單字

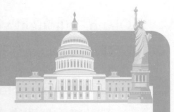

grocery	[ˈgrosərɪ]	名 雜貨
clothes	[kloðz]	名 衣物
next	[nɛkst]	形 下一個
plan	[plæn]	動 計畫
hike	[haɪk]	動 遠足；步行
exercise	[ˈɛksəˌsaɪz]	名 運動

UNIT 24

I'm going to make it an early night.

MP3-25

今晚我要提早離開。

Dialogue 1

A : I'm going to make it an early night.

我要提早離開結束。

B : You're not leaving already, are you?

你還沒要走吧？

A : I've got an 8:00 meeting tomorrow.
I really should look over my work and hit the hay.

我明天早上八點有個會議。

我真的應該要把我的工作看過一遍，然後去睡覺。

B : All right. Thanks for coming.

好的。謝謝你來。

Dialogue 2

A : I'm going to leave this here for Mr. Lee.

我要把這個東西留在這裏給李先生。

B : Is he expecting this package?

他在等這個包裹嗎？

A : Yes, ma'am.

If you could just tell him that John left it for him.

是的。你就告訴他說這是約翰留給他的。

B : No problem, John.

Have a good day.

沒問題，約翰。

祝你有美好的一天。

單字

early	['ɝlɪ]	副 早
leave	[liv]	動 離開
meeting	['mitɪŋ]	名 會議
hit	[hɪt]	動 撞
expect	[ɪk'spɛkt]	動 預期；期待
package	['pækɪdʒ]	名 包裹
problem	['prɑbləm]	名 問題

UNIT 25 | May is going to travel around the world.

MP3-26

梅要去環遊世界。

Dialogue 1

A : I heard May is going to travel around the world.

我聽說梅要去環遊世界。

B : Yeah, I heard that too.
It must be nice.

是啊，我也聽說了。

那一定很棒。

A : No kidding. I'd love to have nothing to do but travel.

就是說嘛！我喜歡除了旅行什麼都不做的生活。

B : You will one day.
Tell May to send us plenty of postcards.

有一天你可以做到的。

叫梅多寄一些明信片給我們。

Dialogue 2

A : Did you know that Henry is going to leave after the end of the year?

　　你知道亨利年底之後要離開嗎？

B : No, where did you hear that?

　　不知道，你從哪裏聽來的？

A : From Henry himself.
He found another job.

　　亨利自己說的。
　　他找到另一個工作了。

B : Oh man, I really like him.

　　哦！老兄，我真的很喜歡他。

心靈雞湯

Turn on your headlights when it begins to rain.
開始下雨時，請打開你的車前燈。

單字

travel	['trævl̩]	動 旅行
around	[ə'raʊnd]	副 （時間）前後；大約
world	[wɝld]	名 世界
postcard	['postkɑrd]	名 明信片
another	[ə'nʌðɚ]	形 另一個
job	[dʒɑb]	名 工作；職位

心靈雞湯

Read more books, watch less TV.
多閱讀，少看電視。

MP3-27

UNIT 26
What are you going to wear to the party?

你打算穿什麼去參加派對？

Dialogue 1

A : What are you going to wear to the party?

你打算穿什麼去參加派對？。

B : I haven't decided.
I have a black dress and a blue one.
How about you?

我還沒決定。
我有一件黑色的衣服還有一件藍色的。
你呢？

A : I'm wearing the same one I wore to your Christmas party last year.

我要穿去年去你的聖誕派對穿的那一件。

B : Oh that's a gorgeous dress!
You'll look great!

哦，那件衣服很漂亮！
你穿起來會很好看！

Dialogue 2

A ： I haven't got a tuxedo.
What are you going to wear to the party?

我沒有燕尾服。
你要穿什麼衣服去派對？

B ： I don't have a tuxedo, either.
I'm just going to wear a nice suit.

我也沒有燕尾服。
我就打算穿一件好一點的西裝。

A ： That would be okay?

那樣可以嗎？

B ： Oh yes, the party isn't that formal.

哦，可以，這派對沒有那麼正式。

心靈雞湯

Use credit cards only for convenience,
never for credit.
請為了便利性，使用信用卡，而不是
為了賒帳。

單字

wear	[wɛr]	動 穿
decide	[dɪˈsaɪd]	動 決定
wore	[wor]	動 穿；戴（wear 的過去式）
gorgeous	[ˈgɔrdʒəs]	形 （口語）很美好的
suit	[sut]	名 西裝
formal	[ˈfɔrml̩]	形 正式的

生活小忠告

Fill your gas tank when it falls below one-quarter full.

當你的油箱低於四分之一滿時，請加滿油。

UNIT 27 | Are you going to grade those papers tonight?

MP3-28

你今晚要打那些報告的分數嗎？

Dialogue 1

A : Are you going to grade those papers tonight?

你今晚要打那些報告的分數嗎？

B : Yes, I have to.
I'm really behind.
What are you doing tonight?

是的，我不做不行了。
我的進度真的落後了。
你今晚要做什麼？

A : Reading mostly.
Can I give you a lift?

主要是讀書吧。
要我載你一程嗎？

B : Yeah I'd appreciate that, thanks.

好啊，感激不盡，謝謝。

Dialogue 2

A : Are you going to the game tonight?
你今晚要去看比賽嗎？

B : Oh yeah, I wouldn't miss it. Are you?
哦，是啊，我不會錯過的。你呢？

A : Absolutely. Do you want to meet there?
當然要去呀。你想要在那裏碰面嗎？

B : That would be great.
I'll see you at the main gate.
那樣很好。
我就和你在大門口處見面。

心靈雞湯

Buy great books, even if you never read them.
去買一些好書，就算你從未閱讀它們。

單字

grade	[gred]	動 打成績
paper	['pepɚ]	名 研究報告
behind	[bɪ'haɪnd]	介 落後
mostly	['mostlɪ]	副 大半
appreciate	[ə'priʃɪ,et]	動 感激
miss	[mɪs]	動 想念；錯過
main	[men]	形 主要的
gate	[get]	名 大門

UNIT 28 | It's going to rain.

快要下雨了。

Dialogue 1

A : Look at those clouds.

It's going to rain.

看看那些雲。

快要下雨了。

B: Don't say that.

I want to run in the sunshine for a day.

別這麼說。

我希望能今天能在陽光下跑跑步。

A : Well, I don't think it will be today.

The weatherman agrees with my forecast.

嗯，我不認為你今天可以。

氣象播報員也同意我的預測。

B : Man, I'm going to get sick running in this rain.

老兄，我會因為在這場這雨中跑步而生病了。

Dialogue 2

A : It's going to be a beautiful day today.

今天會是美麗的一天。

B : Tell me about it.

Do you want to go on a picnic or something?

還用你說。

你想要去野餐或做些什麼事嗎？

A : I haven't gone a picnic since I was a kid.

從我長大以後我就沒野餐過了。

B : Well, let's do it then.

嗯，那我們就去野餐吧。

單字

cloud	[klaʊd]	名 雲
sunshine	[ˈsʌnˌʃaɪn]	名 陽光
weatherman	[ˈwɛðəˌmæn]	名 氣象預報員
forecast	[ˈforˌkæst]	名 預測
picnic	[ˈpɪknɪk]	名 野餐

UNIT 29 | He is going to be late for the meeting.

他開會會晚到。

Dialogue 1

A : Tell Mr. White, that Rob is going to be late for the meeting.

告訴懷特先生，羅伯開會會晚到。

B : How late?

多晚？

A : He said as soon as his client finishes looking at the property, he will leave for the office.

他說一旦他的客戶看完房子之後，他就會立刻來公司。

B : Okay I'll tell White.

好的，我會告訴懷特。

Dialogue 2

A : He is going to miss his plane if he doesn't hurry.

他如果不快一點他就要趕不上飛機了。

B ： Don't worry, he'll be on time.
He always is.

> 別擔心，他會準時到的。
> 他總是如此。

A ： Well, he's not on time now.
He should've been here thirty minutes ago.

> 嗯，他現在就不準時了。
> 三十分鐘前他就應該到了。

B ： I told you to relax.
Look, here he comes now.

> 我說了，放輕鬆。
> 看，他現在到了。

單字

client	[ˈklaɪənt]	名 客戶
finish	[ˈfɪnɪʃ]	動 完成
property	[ˈprɑpɚtɪ]	名 地產
plane	[plen]	名 飛機
hurry	[ˈhɝɪ]	動 匆忙；趕快
relax	[rɪˈlæks]	動 放輕鬆

UNIT 30 — I think I'll take the train into the city.

MP3-31

我想我會搭火車進城。

Dialogue 1

A : Well, if you're going back to work, I think I'll take a taxi back to the apartment.

嗯，如果你要回去工作，我想我會搭計程車回公寓。

B : Okay. Thanks for lunch.

好的。謝謝你的午餐。

A : My pleasure. So I'll see you tonight?

這是我的榮幸。那麼今晚見？

B : Yep. I'll be at your place around 7:00.

是的。我大約七點到你那裏。

Dialogue 2

A : I think I'll take the train into the city.
It's been a while since I've ridden the train.

我想我會搭火車進城。
我已經好一陣整子沒有搭火車了。

B： Do you have money for the fare?

你有錢付車票嗎？

A： Yes, I have plenty of money.

Did you want anything from the city?

有，我有很多錢。

你要我從城裏買什麼東西給你嗎？

B： No thanks.

I'll be up there Monday if I need anything.

不，謝謝。

如果我需要什麼的話，我星期一會上去那裏。

單字

back	[bæk]	副 回來
apartment	[ə'pɑrtmənt]	名 公寓
pleasure	['plɛʒɚ]	名 榮幸
fare	[fɛr]	名 車資
train	[tren]	名 火車

MP3-32

UNIT
31 | # I think I'll stay home tonight.

我想我今晚會待在家裏。

Dialogue 1

A : I think I'll stay home tonight.
我想我今晚會待在家裏。

B : Why? Don't you want to see your friends?
為什麼？你不想出去看朋友嗎？

A : I see them everyday.
I just want some quiet time to myself.
我每天都會見到他們。
我只是想給自己一些安靜的時間。

B : Well, that's understandable.
I like some private time, too.
嗯，可以理解。
我也想要有有一些私人的時間。

Dialogue 2

A : What are you doing this weekend?
你這個週末要做什麼？

B : I think I'll finally clean my house.
我想我終於要清理我的房子了。

A : That sounds like fun.
See you on Monday.
那聽起來很有趣。
週一見了。

B : Have a good weekend.
週末愉快。

單字

quiet	[ˈkwaɪət]	形 安靜的
understandable	[ˌʌndɚˈstændəbḷ]	形 可以理解的
private	[ˈpraɪvɪt]	形 私人的
finally	[ˈfaɪnḷɪ]	副 最終；終於
clean	[klin]	動 清理

UNIT 32 I'll help you with that bag if it's too heavy.

如果那個袋子太重，我可以幫你。

Dialogue 1

A : I'll help you with that bag if it's too heavy.

如果那個袋子太重，我可以幫你提。

B : Thanks. It is a bit heavy.

謝謝。它是有一點重。

A : You must have packed a lot of clothes.

你一定是裝了一大堆衣服。

B : I always over-pack.

我總是裝得太多。

Dialogue 2

A : I'll help you with that project if you want me to.

如果你想要我幫你做那份企畫的話，我可以幫你做。

B ： That would be great, Jill, thank you.

那真是太好了，吉兒，謝謝。

A ： I've got some free time after lunch.
Let's get together then.

我午餐後會有一些空閒時間。

我們就那個時候碰面吧。

B ： Wonderful. I'll be here around 1:00.

太好了。我大約一點會到這裏。

單字

bag	[bæg]	名 袋子
heavy	[ˈhɛvɪ]	形 重的
pack	[pæk]	動 裝箱
always	[ˈɔlwez]	副 總是
project	[ˈprɑdʒɛkt]	名 專案；企畫
free	[fri]	形 有空的
wonderful	[ˈwʌndɚfəl]	形 好棒的；絕妙的；好極了

UNIT 33 I'll show you.

MP3-34

我帶你去。

Dialogue 1

A : Could you tell me where the restrooms are?

你可以告訴我洗手間在哪裏嗎？

B : They're in the back.

I'll show you.

在後面。

我帶你去。

A : Thanks. I don't know if I would've found them.

謝謝。我不知道我自己是否找得到。

B : No problem. Glad I could help.

沒問題。我很高興能幫忙。

英文裡的 baby sitter，就是保母。

Dialogue 2

A : Do you know where room 2553 is?

你知道 **2553** 號房在哪裏嗎？

B : Yes, I'll show you where it is.

It would be easier than telling you.

知道，我帶你去。

那比告訴你在哪還容易。

A : This building is confusing.

這座樓很令人困惑。

B : Yes, I know.

It took me a while to figure it out.

Here you go – 2553.

是的，我知道。

我花了好一陣子才弄清楚它。

到了－ **2553**。

心靈雞湯

Overpay for a good baby sitter.

給一個好保母較高的薪資

單字

back	[bæk]	名 後面
problem	[ˈprɑbləm]	名 問題
show	[ʃo]	動 帶 (某人) 去
building	[ˈbɪldɪŋ]	名 大樓
confusing	[kənˈfjuʒən]	形 令人困惑
figure out	[ˈfɪgjɚ]	片 弄清楚

UNIT 34 | I'll pay you back tomorrow.

MP3-35

我明天還你。

Dialogue 1

A : Could I borrow $20?

我可以跟和你借 **20** 元嗎？

B : Sure. Here you go.

當然。拿去。

A : Thanks for lending me the money.
I'll pay you back tomorrow.

謝謝你借我錢。
我明天還你。

B : Don't worry about it.

別在意。

Dialogue 2

A : Do you have that $100 you owe me?
I could use it.

你有錢還欠我的 **100** 元嗎？
我需要用。

B : I don't have it with me now, but I'll pay you tomorrow.

我現在沒有錢還你，但是我明天會還你。

A : That's fine.
Just don't forget.

沒問題。

只是別忘了。

B : I won't.
I'll have it for you tomorrow morning.

我不會的。我明天早上還你。

單字

borrow	[ˈbɑro]	動 借用
lend	[lɛnd]	動 借
pay	[pe]	動 付錢
owe	[o]	動 虧欠
forget	[fɚˈgɛt]	動 忘記

UNIT 35 | The car won't start.

MP3-36

車子發不動。

Dialogue 1

A : I don't believe this.
The car won't start.

      我不敢相信。
      車子發不動。

B : You're kidding.
What do we do now?

      你在開玩笑吧。
      現在我們要怎麼辦？

A : I guess we should call a cab.
We can't be late.

      我想我們應該叫計程車。
      我們不能遲到。

B : Okay, I'll go call a cab.

      好的，我來叫計程車。

Dialogue 2

A : Lisa won't go to the meeting.

麗莎不會來參加會議。

B : Why not?

為什麼不來？

A : She says that she won't go to a meeting over the weekend.

她說她週末不出席會議。

B : Ask her to come in here for a minute.

叫她到我辦公室來一會兒。

單字

believe	[bɪˈliv]	動 相信
start	[stɑrt]	動 啟動（車子）
cab	[kæb]	名 計程車
guess	[gɛs]	動 猜想
meeting	[ˈmitɪŋ]	名 會議

MP3-37

UNIT 36

I won't tell anyone.

我不會告訴任何人

Dialogue 1

A : Now this is a secret.
So you can't tell anyone.

這可是一個秘密。

你不能告訴任何人。

- -

B : Don't worry. I won't tell anyone what you said.

別擔心，我不會告訴任何人你說的事。

- -

A : Not even your wife.

連你的太太都不能說。

- -

B : I promise I won't tell anyone, not even my wife.

我保證我不會告訴任何人，連我的太太我也不會告訴她。

- -

Dialogue 2

A : What are you going to say on the stand?

你作證時要說什麼？

- -

B： I won't lie about what happened.
I'll be under oath.

關於發生的事情，我不會說謊。
我做證時，得宣示要說實話的。

A： Yes, you will.
Well, good luck.

是的。
那，祝好運。

B： Thanks. I'll see you later.
謝謝。稍晚見。

單字

secret	[ˈsikrɪt]	名 秘密
even	[ˈivən]	副 甚至
promise	[ˈprɑmɪs]	動 承諾；保證；答應
stand	[stænd]	名 證人台
lie	[laɪ]	動 說謊
happen	[ˈhæpən]	動 發生
oath	[oθ]	名 誓言

UNIT 37 | I bet Mary will get the job. 我打賭瑪麗會得到那個工作。

MP3-38

Dialogue 1

A : Did you hear about that supervisor position opening up?

你有聽說那個主管的職位公開徵求中嗎？

B : Yes, I bet Mary will get the job.

有的，我打賭瑪麗會得到那個工作。

A : You're right she probably will.
I think I'll apply anyway though.

你說的沒錯，她可能會。

雖然如此，無論如何我想我還是會去應徵。

B : Do that.
You have as much a chance as anyone.

去做吧。

你和任何人有一樣多的機會。

Dialogue 2

A : The investors decided to back out of the deal.
投資者決定退出計畫。

B : John will not be happy about that.
約翰會不高興的。

A : Yeah, I know.
I get to tell him about it.
我知道他會不高興。
我會找機會告訴他這件事。

B : I'm glad I'm not in your shoes. Good luck.
我很高興我不是你。祝好運。

心靈雞湯

Remember that creating a successful marriage is like farming.
記得，創造一個成功的婚姻就像是耕田一樣。

單字

supervisor	[supɚˈvaɪzɚ]	名 主管
position	[pəˈzɪʃən]	名 職位
bet	[bɛt]	動 打賭
probably	[ˈprɑbəblɪ]	副 或許；可能的
though	[ðo]	副 （口語）不過
chance	[tʃæns]	名 機會
investor	[ɪnˈvɛstɚ]	名 投資者
deal	[dil]	名 交易

UNIT 38 | I guess I'll see you next week.

我想我們下週見了。

Dialogue 1

A : Well, we're done here.
Thanks for stopping by.

> 嗯，我們做完了。
> 謝謝你過來。

B : So I guess I'll see you next week.

> 我想我們下週見了。

A : Yes, you will.
Bright and early on Tuesday morning.

> 是的。星期二一大早。

B : I'll be here. Thanks.

> 我會來的。謝謝。

Dialogue 2

A : I guess I'll clean the house now.
I've been lazy all day.

> 我想我現在要清理房屋了。
> 我已經偷懶了一天。

B : Can I help you do anything?

　　　我可以幫你做些什麼嗎？

A : You don't have to help.
　　　I'll clean. Go enjoy the movie.

　　　你不用幫忙。
　　　我會清理。去享受電影吧。

B : Let me know if you change your mind.

　　　如果你改變主意了請讓我知道。

單字

guess	[gɛs]	動 猜想
bright	[braɪt]	形 天亮的
early	[ˈɝlɪ]	副 早
clean	[klin]	動 清潔的
lazy	[ˈlezɪ]	形 怠惰的
enjoy	[ɪnˈdʒɔɪ]	動 享受
mind	[maɪnd]	名 想法

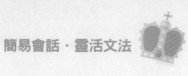

MEMO

CHAPTER 4

Shall 和 Will 的用法

本章要告訴各位 will 和 shall 的用法。

will 是表示「未來」的助動詞,也可以用來要求對方做某件事。

shall 則是用來問對方:「你要我這麼做嗎?」或是問:「我們要做什麼呢?」

本章還要告訴大家,如何使用「未來進行式」。

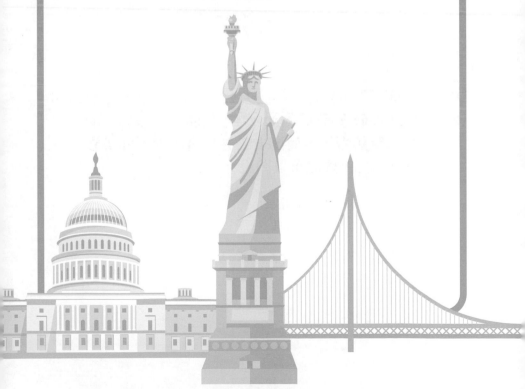

A 當你想要對方幫你做什麼事的時候，你可以說 **Will you** 幫我做這件事，例如：有人走進門來，沒有把門關上，一股冷風直吹進來，你跟對方說，請把門關上，英語就是：

Will you shut the door?
　　（可以請你關門嗎？）

同樣這句話，客氣一點的說法是：
Would you please shut the door?

B 要告訴對方說，我知道你會這樣的，英語就是 **You'll**…，例如：約翰擔心他考試會考不及格，於是你安慰他說，不會的，你會考及格的，英語就是：

Don't worry. You'll pass.

C 有件事你不知道該不該去做，你就該問對方說 **Shall I...?** 去做這件事，例如：你到朋友家作客，朋友家的電話鈴響了，而朋友正在忙著，你不知道該不該去接電話，你就可以問說，

Shall I answer the phone?
　　（我應該去接電話嗎？）

這句話含有，「你要我去接電話嗎」的意思。

UNIT 39 | Will you get that book for me?

MP3-40

你可以幫我拿那本書嗎？

Dialogue 1

A ： Will you bring these boxes to the garage?
你可以把這些箱子拿去車庫嗎？

B ： How many are there?
有幾個？

A ： About twenty.
I just want them in the garage and out of the way.
大概二十個。
我只是想要把它們放在車庫，以免擋路。

B ： Sure. Where are they?
好的。它們在哪裏？

Dialogue 2

A : Will you get that book for me?

你可以幫我拿那本書嗎？

B : What's the matter, shorty?

怎麼啦，矮子？

A : Very funny.

The red one on the top shelf.

別耍幽默。

在最上層那本紅色的。

B : There you go.

拿去吧。

單字

garage	[gə'rɑʒ]	名	車庫
matter	['mætɚ]	名	事情
funny	['fʌnɪ]	形	可笑的
shelf	[ʃɛlf]	名	架子

UNIT 40 | Will you shut the door, please?

MP3-41

可以請你關門嗎？

Dialogue 1

A : Will you shut the door, please?

可以請你關門嗎？

B : Sorry, I didn't realize it was open.

抱歉，我不知道它是開著的。

A : It wasn't you.
The door is just difficult to close completely.

不是你的關係。

那扇門就是很難完全關上。

B : Yes, it is.

沒錯。

Dialogue 2

A : John, will you turn the television down?
約翰，可以把電視關小聲嗎？

B : Yeah. Are you studying or something?
可以啊。你要唸書還是做什麼？

A : No, I'm on the phone with Tina.
不是，我在和蒂娜講電話。

B : Oh, sorry. Tell Tina I said hello.
哦，抱歉。幫我和蒂娜問好。

單字

shut	[ʃʌt]	動 關
realize	[ˈriə‚laɪz]	動 明瞭；知道
difficult	[ˈdɪfə‚kʌlt]	形 困難的
completely	[kəmˈplitlɪ]	副 完全地
phone	[fon]	名 電話

UNIT 41 | Will you please be quiet?

MP3-42

可以請你安靜點嗎？

Dialogue 1

A : Will you please be quiet?

可以請你安靜點嗎？

B : I thought I was being quiet.

我以為我很安靜了。

A : You're not being quiet if I can hear everything you're saying.

如果我可以聽到你所說的每句話，就表示你並不安靜。

B : Okay, I'll just go to another room.

好的，我會到另一間房間去。

Dialogue 2

A : Will you please be quiet?
I have a huge headache.

可以請你安靜點嗎？
我頭痛的很嚴重。

B : I'm sorry.

Would you like some aspirin?

抱歉。

你想要吃一些阿斯匹靈嗎？

A : I already took some.

I just need to lie down and be left quiet.

我已經吃了一些了。

我只需要躺下來安靜一下。

B : Absolutely. Let me know if you need anything.

沒錯。如果你需要任何東西，讓我知道。

單字

Quiet	[ˈkwaɪət]	形 安靜的
Another	[əˈnʌðɚ]	形 另一個
Room	[rum]	名 房間
Headache	[ˈhɛdˌek]	名 頭痛
Already	[ɔlˈrɛdɪ]	副 已經

UNIT 42 You'll pass.

MP3-43

你會過關的。

Dialogue 1

A : I am so anxious about that test.

我很擔心那個測驗。

B : Don't worry. You'll pass.

別擔心。你會過關的。

A : I don't care anymore.
I just want to get it over with.

我一點也不在乎。
我只想趕快考完。

B : You'll do fine. Stop working yourself up.

你會做的很好的，別把你自己鬧的緊張兮兮的。

Dialogue 2

A : Do you think I'll do okay?
Maybe I should have practiced more.

你認為我會做得好嗎？
也許我應該再多練習一些。

B : You'll be great.

You know your lines backwards and forwards.

你會做得很好的。你的台詞已經背得滾瓜爛熟。

A : I'm so nervous.

我好緊張。

B : That's normal.

You'll be at ease once you get into it.

Go break a leg.

那很正常。

等你開始做的時候你就會感覺輕鬆了。勇敢去做吧。

單字

fine	[faɪn]	形 好的
practice	[ˈpræktɪs]	動 練習
backwards	[ˈbækwɚdz]	副 由後往前
forwards	[ˈfɔrdwɚdz]	副 由前往後
line	[laɪn]	名 台詞
nervous	[ˈnɝvəs]	形 緊張的
normal	[ˈnɔrml̩]	形 正常的
once	[wʌns]	連 一旦

UNIT 43 | Shall I answer the phone?

MP3-44

我應該去接電話嗎？

Dialogue 1

A : Shall I answer the phone?
　　 我應該去接電話嗎？

B : Would you mind?
　　 I've got cookie dough all over my hands.
　　 請你去接好嗎？
　　 我滿手都是做餅乾的麵糰。

A : Hello? Yes, she is, just one moment.
　　 哈囉？是的，她在，請稍等。

B : Thanks. The cookies will be ready in a minute.
　　 謝謝。再一分鐘餅乾很快就好了。

Dialogue 2

A : There's Mom back from the grocery store.
媽媽從雜貨店回來了。

B : Shall I help her with the bags?
我要去幫她提袋子嗎？

A : She'd appreciate that.
她會很感謝的。

B : I would too if I had to carry all that stuff in.
如果我必須提那所有東西進來，我也會感謝的。

單字

mind	[maɪnd]	動 介意
dough	[do]	名 麵糰
ready	[ˈrɛdɪ]	形 準備好
appreciate	[əˈpriʃɪ,et]	動 感激
stuff	[stʌf]	名 東西
carry	[ˈkærɪ]	動 攜帶

UNIT 44 | Shall I close the window?

MP3-45

我要關上窗戶嗎?

Dialogue 1

A : It's chilly in here, isn't it?

這裏面很冷,不是嗎?

B : Yes, it is.
Shall I close the window?

的確是的,很冷。我要關上窗戶嗎?

A : Yes, please.
I think I'll put on a sweater, too.

是的,請關上。我想我也要穿上一件毛衣。

B : Your blue sweater is on the hook if you want that one.

你的藍色毛衣在掛鈎上,如果你要穿那一件的話。

Dialogue 2

A : It's getting late.
Shall I lock all the doors?

天晚了。我要把所有的門都鎖起來嗎?

B ： You can but I don't do that normally.

這可以，不過我通常不那麼做。

A ： Why not?

為什麼不？

B ： This is the country.

It's just not a habit we've developed.

這裏是鄉下。我們不習慣鎖門。

單字

chilly	[ˈtʃɪlɪ]	形 寒冷的
sweater	[ˈswɛtɚ]	名 毛衣
hook	[hʊk]	名 掛鈎
lock	[lɑk]	名 鎖
normally	[ˈnɔrməlɪ]	副 通常；一般來說
country	[ˈkʌntrɪ]	名 鄉下
habit	[ˈhæbɪt]	名 習慣
develop	[dɪˈvɛləp]	動 發展

UNIT 45 | Where shall we go this evening?

MP3-46

今天晚上我們要去哪裏？

Dialogue 1

A : So where shall we go this evening?
那，所以今天晚上我們要去哪裏？

B : Well, I was thinking that maybe we could go see a play.
嗯，我在想也許我們可以去看場表演。

A : There's an idea.
What are our choices?
好主意。
有什麼表演我們可以去看的？

B : Honestly I want to go see Othello.
It's playing at the Marks Theater.
老實說我想去看奧賽羅。
它在馬克斯劇院演出。

Dialogue 2

A : Let's go out tonight.

我們今晚出去吧。

B : I'm game.
Where shall we go?

我有興趣。我們要去哪？

A : I have tickets to the hockey game or we can go grab some dinner.

我有曲棍球賽的票，或者我們可以去吃晚餐。

B : Let's do both.
Dinner and the game.

讓我們兩個都去吧。晚餐和球賽。

單字

idea	[aɪˈdɪə]	名 主意；概念
choice	[tʃɔɪs]	名 選擇
honestly	[ˈɑnəstlɪ]	副 誠實的
ticket	[ˈtɪkɪt]	名 票；單子；交通罰單
hockey	[ˈhɑkɪ]	名 曲棍球

UNIT 46 | Will you be using your computer this evening?

你今晚要用電腦嗎?

Dialogue 1

A : Will you be using your computer this evening?

你今晚要用電腦嗎?

B : I use my computer every evening. Why?

我每天晚上都會用電腦。為什麼這麼問?

A : I was wondering if I could type a paper on it.

我在想我可不可以用來打一篇報告。

B : Oh sure.

Just call me and let me know when you're coming.

哦,沒問題。

打個電話給我,讓我知道你什麼時候要來。

Dialogue 2

A : Will you be home tonight?

你今晚會在家嗎？

B : For a while before I leave for the airport.

在我離開去機場前，我會在家一下子。

A : Is it all right if I come get that book before you go?

我可以在你離開前去拿那本書可以嗎？

B : Sure that's fine.

I'm leaving at 5:30, so you can come over anytime before then.

當然，沒問題。

我五點半離開，所以你可以在那之前的任何時間過來。

單字

computer	[kəmˈpjutɚ]	電腦
type	[taɪp]	動 打字
airport	[ˈɛrˌport]	名 飛機場
leave	[liv]	動 離開

UNIT 47

Will you be passing the post office on your way out?

MP3-48

你出門的路上會經過郵局嗎？

Dialogue 1

A : Will you be passing the post office on your way out?

你出門的路上會經過郵局嗎？

B : Yes, I will.

Do you need anything dropped in the mail?

是的，我會。

你要郵寄任何東西嗎？

A : Yes, I need to mail this package.

Would you mind?

是的，我要寄這個包裹。

你介意幫我寄嗎？

B : Not at all.

我不介意。

Dialogue 2

A : I'm on my way home, Frank.

我正在回家的路上，法蘭克。

B： Will you be stopping by the club on your way home?

你在回家的路上可以去俱樂部一下嗎？

A： Yes, why?

可以啊，你要做什麼？

B： If Steve is there, tell him I'll see him next week.

如果史帝夫在那裏，告訴他我下週會和他見面。

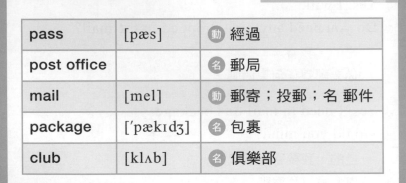

單字

pass	[pæs]	動 經過
post office		名 郵局
mail	[mel]	動 郵寄；投郵；名 郵件
package	[ˈpækɪdʒ]	名 包裹
club	[klʌb]	名 俱樂部

 心靈雞湯

blood 是血液的意思，而 blood type 就是血型。

CHAPTER 5

過去式

過去式原本應該是很容易分辨的，只要是過去發生的事情，就該用過去式。

問題是，中文說到過去的事，可以從說話的前後文去瞭解，或是由表示時間的副詞，自然瞭解到，對方說的是「過去的事情」，中文句子中的動詞不會變。

當你用英文跟別人說：我今天早上起床晚了，因為是今天早上發生的事，在英語裡，要把動詞 get up 改成過去式 got up。

A 句子裡有表示「過去」的時間副詞，例如：昨天，今天早上，去年，上個月，上星期，句子的動詞都要改成過去式。

B 句子裡雖然沒有表示「過去」的時間副詞，但是從說話的前後文裡，知道是在說一件過去的事，句子裡的動詞也要改成過去式。

例如：你打電話給朋友，朋友

來接電話時，你一聽他那還沒睡醒的聲音，就猜到，他是被你的電話聲吵醒的，你就趕緊先問一句：

DidI wake you up?

（我把你吵醒了嗎？）

你有沒有注意到這個句子用的是過去式助動詞 did，因為，不管你有沒有吵醒他，你問的是一件發生在你說話的時候之前的事情。

UNIT 48 | I got up late this morning.

MP3-49

我今天睡過頭了。

Dialogue 1

A : Well, nice of you to show up to work.

嗯，你有來上班真是太好了。

B : I'm sorry, I got up late this morning.

對不起，我今天睡過頭了。

A : No kidding, it's almost 11:00.

別開玩笑了，現在快 **11:00** 了。

B : I know, I know.
The baby was up all night.
I just overslept.

我知道，我知道。
嬰兒一整晚都醒著。
我就睡過頭了。

Dialogue 2

A : Did you finish that article this morning?
你今天早上完成那篇文章了嗎？

B : I had planned on that, but I got up a little late.
我本來有打算那麼做，但是我睡晚了一點。

A : Can you finish it now?
你現在可以完成嗎？

B : Yes, ma'am I'll get right on it.
是的，我現在馬上做。

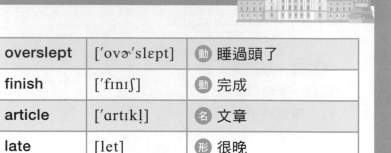

單字

overslept	[ˈovɚˈslɛpt]	動 睡過頭了
finish	[ˈfɪnɪʃ]	動 完成
article	[ˈɑrtɪkḷ]	名 文章
late	[let]	形 很晚

UNIT 49

The weather was good yesterday afternoon.

昨天下午的天氣很好。

MP3-50

Dialogue 1

A : It's too bad the barbecue wasn't yesterday.
The weather was good yesterday afternoon.

烤肉會沒在昨天辦真是太遺憾了。
昨天下午的天氣很好。

B : It was nice yesterday.
Oh well, the bbq is on the covered porch.
It should still taste good.

昨天天氣是很好。
哦，烤肉架是在有頂的走廊下。
應該還是很好吃。

A : I'm sure it will.
You make some good barbecued chicken.

這我相信。
你的烤雞肉一向很好吃。

B : The sausage is my favorite.

我最喜歡的是香腸。

Dialogue 2

A : I cant' believe how beautiful it was yesterday afternoon.
真我不敢相信昨天下午的天氣那麼好。

B : I know, I wanted to work outdoors all day yesterday.
我知道，我希望我昨天一整天都在戶外工作。

A : It figures that now we are off work that weather is bad.
它料到我們現在不用上班，所以天氣就變壞了。

B : That's life.
Let's rent a movie and order pizza.
那就是人生。
我們去租一部電影再叫披薩吧。

單字

weather	[ˈwɛðɚ]	名 天氣
taste	[test]	動 嚐起來
porch	[portʃ]	名 走廊
sausage	[ˈsɔsɪdʒ]	名 香腸
favorite	[ˈfevərɪt]	名 最喜歡的
outdoors	[ˈautˈdorz]	副 戶外
order	[ˈordɚ]	動 訂貨
rent	[rɛnt]	動 租

生活小忠告

Laugh loudly.
笑的開懷。

UNIT 50 | It rained all day yesterday.
昨天下了一整天的雨。

Dialogue 1

A : Did you get a chance to work in your garden?

你有機會在花園裏做些工作嗎？

B : No, it rained all day yesterday.
I didn't get any gardening done.

沒有，昨天下了一整天的雨。
我什麼園藝都沒做。

A : That's too bad.
What did you do all day?

那太糟了。
你一整天都做什麼事？

B : I played with my niece.

我和我的姪女玩。

Dialogue 2

A : I'm glad it rained all day yesterday.
The grass needed it.

　我很高興昨天下了一整天的雨。
　草需要雨水。

B : I know, it's been so dry and hot lately.

　我知道，最近是如此的乾熱。

A : I'm afraid that the heat will burn up all the rain that did fall.

　我怕熱氣會蒸發掉所有的雨水。

B : No, it's supposed to be overcast all day today.
That will give the water a chance to sink into the ground.

　不會，今天一整天應該都是陰天。
　那會讓水分有機會滲入地面。

單字

chance	[tʃæns]	名 機會
garden	[ˈgɑrdn̩]	名 花園
gardening	[ˈgɑrdn̩ɪŋ]	名 園藝
niece	[nis]	名 姪女
grass	[græs]	名 草地
dry	[draɪ]	形 乾的
lately	[ˈletlɪ]	副 近來；最近的
overcast	[ˈovɚˌkæst]	形 （天氣）陰霾的
sink	[sɪŋk]	動 滲入

UNIT 51 | Where were you yesterday?

MP3-52

你昨天在哪裏？

Dialogue 1

A : Where were you yesterday?

We missed you at the meeting.

你昨天在哪裏？

昨天會議裡沒看到你。

B : I know, I'm sorry.

I wasn't feeling well yesterday.

我知道，對不起。

我昨天身體不舒服。

A : I'm sorry.

Are you better today?

真遺憾。

你今天好點了嗎？

B : Yes, I feel a lot better, thanks.

是的，我感覺好多了，謝謝。

Dialogue 2

A ： What did John say about the trip yesterday?

關於旅行的事昨天約翰怎麼說？

B ： I don't know.
I wasn't here yesterday.

我不知道。我昨天不在這裏。

A ： You too huh?
I was in bed sick.　How about you?

你也是啊？我臥病在床。你呢？

B ： The same. Sick as a dog.
I'm still getting over it.

一樣。病得像條狗。
我還在恢復當中。

單字

miss	[mɪs]	動 錯過
better	[ˈbɛtɚ]	形 較好的
trip	[trɪp]	名 旅程；旅遊
sick	[sɪk]	形 生病；不舒服

UNIT 52 | I didn't go to work yesterday.

MP3-53

我昨天沒有去上班。

Dialogue 1

A : Did you ask your boss for next week off?

你跟你的老闆要求下週要請假了嗎？

B : I didn't get a chance to.
I didn't go to work yesterday.

我沒有機會說。
我昨天沒去上班。

A : Why not?

為什麼沒有？

B : I had jury duty.

我去當陪審團了。

Dialogue 2

A : How was your Friday?

你週五過得如何？

B : Pretty unproductive.
I didn't go to work yesterday.
I was sick.

什麼事也沒做。
我昨天沒有去上班。
我生病了。

A : That's too bad.
How are you today?

那太糟了。
你今天如何？

B : I'm getting better, but I don't want to push it.
我好多了，但是我不想要勉強。

單字

boss	[bɔs]	名 主管；老闆
chance	[tʃæns]	名 機會
jury	[ˈdʒʊərɪ]	名 陪審團
push	[pʊʃ]	動 推

UNIT 53 | What did you do last night?

你昨晚在做什麼？

Dialogue 1

A : What did you do last night?

你昨晚在做什麼？

B : I went to see Star Wars.
I didn't enjoy it.

我去看了星際大戰。
我不喜歡它。

A : You didn't enjoy Star Wars? Why not?

你不喜歡星際大戰？為什麼？

B : I've read all the books.
I guess I just enjoy the books more.

我讀過它所有的書。
我想我只是比較喜歡書。

Dialogue 2

A : What movie did you see?

你看了什麼電影？

B : I went to see Blade.
It was pretty gory.

　　我去看了刀鋒戰士。
　　那真的很殘酷。

A : I saw that, too.
It was pretty bloody.

　　我也看了。
　　它非常血腥。

B : I don't normally like movies like that, but I liked this one.

　　我通常不喜歡那樣的電影，但是我喜歡這一部。

單字

enjoy	[ɪnˈdʒɔɪ]	動 享受；喜歡
movie	[ˈmuvɪ]	名 電影
gory	[ˈgorɪ]	形 血腥的
pretty	[ˈprɪtɪ]	副 非常；相當
bloody	[ˈblʌdɪ]	形 血淋淋的

UNIT 54 | Was the food good?

MP3-55

東西好吃嗎？

Dialogue 1

A : We went to Alfonso's last night.

我們昨晚去 **Alfonso's** 餐廳。

B : Really, was the food good?

真的，東西好吃嗎？

A : It was great.
I haven't had Italian food like that since I lived in Chicago.

很棒。
自從我住在芝加哥後我就沒吃過像那樣的義大利菜了。

B : Maybe I'll go one of these nights with my wife.

也許我這幾天會找一晚和我太太一起去。

Dialogue 2

A : What did you and Stella do last night?

你和史黛拉昨晚在做什麼？

B : We ate dinner at her mother's house.

我們在她媽媽家吃晚餐。

A : Was the food good?

東西好吃嗎？

B : It was terrible.

I'm so glad Stella cooks better than her mother.

很糟。

我真高興史黛拉的廚藝比她媽媽好。

單字

terrible	[ˈtɛrəbl̩]	形 （口語）糟透的
glad	[glæd]	形 高興；樂意；欣慰
cook	[kʊk]	動 烹調；煮

UNIT 55 | I went to see a movie last night.

我昨晚去看了場電影。

MP3-56

Dialogue 1

A : I went to the symphony for the first time last night.
我昨天晚上第一次去聽交響樂。

B : Did you go alone?
你一個人去嗎？

A : Oh no, my brother went with me.
哦，不，我哥哥和我哥哥一起去。

B : That's good.
The symphony hall downtown can be a scary place at night.
那很好。
城裏的交響樂廳晚上是一個可怕的地方。

Dialogue 2

A : I went to see a movie last night.

我昨晚去看了場電影。

B : Did you go alone?

你一個人去嗎？

A : Yes, sometimes I like to go out by myself.

是的，有時候我喜歡自己一個人出門。

B : I can't stand going out alone.

我沒辦法忍受單獨出門。

單字

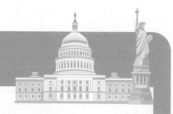

symphony	[ˈsɪmfənɪ]	名 交響樂
alone	[əˈlon]	形 單獨的；獨自
downtown	[ˈdaʊnˈtaʊn]	名 市區；市中心
scary	[ˈskɛrɪ]	形 恐怖的
stand	[stænd]	動 忍受

UNIT 56 | Did you hear about John? 你聽說約翰的事了嗎？

MP3-57

Dialogue 1

A : Did you hear about John?

你聽說約翰的事了嗎？

B : No, what about him?

沒有，他發生什麼事了？

A : He has bone cancer.
He's being hospitalized today.

他得了骨癌。
他今天去住院了。

B : That's terrible.
Let's all go see him.

真是不幸。我們全部去看他吧。

Dialogue 2

A : Hey, did you hear about Steven?
He's moving to Tulsa.

嗨，你聽說史帝芬的事嗎？
他要搬去突沙市了。

B：Why is he doing that?

他為什麼要那樣做？

A：He got a job offer up there that will double his salary.

他在那裏找到一份工作，薪水是現在的兩倍。

B：Well, you can't turn that down.

嗯，你無法拒絕那種事。

單字

cancer	['kænsɚ]	名	癌；癌症
bone	[bon]	名	骨頭
hospitalize	['hɑspɪtl̩,aɪz]	動	入院
offer	['ɔfɚ]	動	提供
double	['dʌbl̩]	動	二倍
salary	['sælərɪ]	名	薪水

UNIT 57 | Did you see John this morning?

MP3-58

你今天早上有看到約翰嗎?

Dialogue 1

A : Did you see John this morning?

你今天早上有看到約翰了嗎?

B : No, I didn't.

He might be in his office now.

沒有。

他現在可能在他的辦公室裏。

A : No, he isn't. I was just there.

If you see him, tell him I'm looking for him.

沒有,他不在,我剛去過那裏。

如果你看到他,告訴他我在找他。

B : Sure thing.

我會的。

Dialogue 2

A : Were you here to open the store this morning?

今天早上是你來開的門嗎？

B : Yes, as always. Why?

是的，就跟往常一樣。怎麼了？

A : Did you see Mary?

你有看到瑪麗嗎？

B : I did.

She came in to say that she wasn't feeling well, then she left for home.

有。

她來說她身體不太舒服，然後就離開回家了。

單字		
office	[ˈɔfɪs]	名 辦公室
store	[stor]	名 商店
well	[wɛl]	形 健康的
left	[lɛft]	動 離開（leave 的過去式）

UNIT 58 | Why didn't you call me last night?

MP3-59

你昨晚為什麼沒有打電話給我？

Dialogue 1

A : Hey John! Why didn't you call me last night?
嘿，約翰！你昨天晚上為什麼沒有打電話給我？

B : I'm sorry, Jane.
I was tied up on the phone with my mother all night.
對不起，珍。
我整個晚上都在和我媽媽講電話。

A : What were you guys talking about all night?
你們兩個一整個晚上在聊些什麼？

B : You know mothers.
We haven't talked in a while, so we were catching up.
你知道媽媽就是那樣。
我們有一段時間沒有聊天了，所以我們在問彼此的近況。

Dialogue 2

A ： Hi Peter.

Why didn't you call me last night?

嗨，彼得，你昨天晚上為什麼沒有打電話給我？

B ： I was at work until 7:00, and then I had to pick up my son.

I'm sorry.

我一直工作到七點，然後我必須去接我兒子。

我很抱歉。

A ： It's all right.

I was just wondering what happened.

沒關係。

我只是在想發生了什麼事。

B ： I promise I will call you tonight.

我保證我今天晚上會打電話給你。

Love deeply.

愛的深切。

單字

phone	[fon]	名 電話
guy	[gaɪ]	名（口語）個人
while	[hwaɪl]	名 一段時間
happen	['hæpən]	動 發生
promise	['prɑmɪs]	動 承諾；保證；答應

心靈雞湯

Surprise an old friend with a phone call.
打個電話，給老朋友一個驚喜。

MEMO

CHAPTER 6

過去進行式

第一章裡，我們學過「現在進行式」的用法，就是在說一件現在正在進行的事，由此類推，可以知道，過去進行式就是在說：「過去的某個時間正在進行的事。」

A 在過去某個時間，某人正在做某件事，要用過去進行式。

例如：你要告訴對方，昨晚十點的時候，你正在寫報告，英語就是：

I was working on my paper at 10:00 last night.

又如：你想知道約翰昨天八點的時候在做什麼，你就問約翰，

What were you doing at 8:00 yesterday?

B 過去進行式，也可以用在：「你所知道的某個時間，某人正在做什麼」。

例如：有人問你昨天早上你離開家的時候，約翰正在做什麼，你回答，我離開家的時候：

John was eating his breakfast.

（約翰正在吃早餐。）

MEMO

UNIT 59 | I fell asleep when I was watching TV.

MP3-60

我看電視看到睡著了。

Dialogue 1

A : My back is killing me.
I should've gone to bed last night.

我背痛的要命。
我昨天晚上應該上床睡覺。

B : Why didn't you go to bed?

你昨天為什麼沒有上床睡覺？

A : I fell asleep when I was watching TV.

我看電視看到睡著了。

B : That's not a good habit to get into.

那不是一個值得養成的好習慣。

Dialogue 2

A : I was so tired last I fell asleep while I was watching TV.

我太累了，所以看電視看到睡著了。

B ： I hate it when I do that.

我討厭這樣做。

A ： Tell me about it.

I woke up with my face in a sandwich.

還用你說。

我起來時我的臉沾滿了三明治。

B ： Maybe you should go to bed and get some rest.

也許你應該上床去休息一下。

單字

back	[bæk]	名 背部
asleep	[ə'slip]	形 睡著的
habit	['hæbɪt]	名 習慣
tired	[taɪrd]	形 疲倦的
sandwich	['sænwɪtʃ]	名 三明治
rest	[rɛst]	名 休息

UNIT 60

When Mary arrived, we were having dinner.

MP3-61

當瑪麗到的時候，我們正在吃晚餐。

Dialogue 1

A : What happened last night after I left?

昨天晚上我離開後發生了什麼事？

B : Well, when Mary arrived, we were having dinner.
She was furious that we had eaten without her.

嗯，當瑪麗到的時候，我們正在吃晚餐。
她因為我們不等她就先開動而大發雷霆。

A : Was she drunk again?

她又喝醉了嗎？

B : Naturally.
Bill had to calm her down and take her home.

當然。
比爾必須讓她冷靜下來，然後送她回家。

163

Dialogue 2

A : Did Mary ever make it over for dinner?
　　瑪麗有沒有來吃晚餐嗎？

B : Actually, Mary arrived when we were having dinner.
　　事實上在我們正在用晚餐的時候瑪麗才到。

A : She is always late.
　　她總是遲到。

B : Yes, but it was no big deal.
　　She sat down and joined in.
　　　是的，但是那沒什麼關係。
　　　她坐下來加入我們。

生 活 小 忠 告

Choose work that is in harmony
with your values.
　選擇一份和你的價值觀相符
的工作。

單字

arrive	[əˈraɪv]	動 抵達
furious	[ˈfjʊrɪəs]	形 憤怒的
drunk	[drʌŋk]	形 酒醉的
again	[əˈgen]	副 再度；又
calm	[kɑm]	形 冷靜；平靜
join	[dʒɔɪn]	動 加入

MEMO

MEMO

CHAPTER 7

現在完成式

過去式用來陳述：「過去發生的事情」，現在完
成式也是在陳述：「過去發生的事情」，但指的
是「持續到現在」的事情。

例如：你找不到約翰，你問別人說，Have you seen John this morning? 這句話表明，問這句話的時間仍然在早上。

你如果問：Did you see John this morning?

問這句話的時間已經過了中午。

A 事情發生了，而且持續到現在，就要用現在完成式。

例如：車子不動了，你說：「我想是沒汽油了」，因為「汽油用完了」，這件事持續到現在，英語的說法是：

The car has run out of gas.

（車子的汽油用完了。）

如果你跟朋友說：昨天在上班的途中，「汽油用完了」。英語的說法就是，

The car ran out of gas. 因為你是在述說一件昨天（過去發生）的事。

B 現在完成式常常跟 just 和 already 這兩個副詞一起用，just 表示這件事剛剛過去，有持續到接近現在的意思，常用現在完成式。

例如：大夥兒要去吃午飯，邀你一起去吃，你說：「我剛吃過午飯」，我就不跟你們去吃了，英語就是：

I've just had lunch.

（我才剛吃過午飯。）

already 是「已經」的意思，用現在完成式與 already 一起用，是表示「事情比預期的要早發生」的意思，例如：約翰提醒你要寄某封信，你回答說，我已經寄出去了，英語的說法就是，

I've already mailed it.

UNIT 61 It looks like it has run out of gas.

MP3-62

我想車子的汽油用完了。

Dialogue 1

A : What's the matter with the car?

車子怎麼啦？

B : I think the car has run out of gas.

我想車子的汽油用完了。

A : Run out of gas?
You didn't fill up before we left?

汽油用完了？
我們離開前你沒有加滿嗎？

B : Well, I didn't think we'd be driving for very long.

嗯，我以為我們不會開很遠。

Dialogue 2

A : What's going on with that car?

車子怎麼了？

B： It looks like it has run out of gas.

它看起來像是油用完了。

A： I've got a gas can in my car.

Let's go fill it up with some gas.

我車子裏有一個油桶。

我們去買一些汽油。

B： Okay. There's a station on the corner.

Let's go.

好的。轉角有一個加油站。

走吧。

單字

gas	[gæs]	名 汽油
can	[kæn]	名 桶
fill up		片 加滿（汽油等）
station	[ˈsteʃən]	名 加油站
corner	[ˈkɔrnɚ]	名 角落

UNIT 62 | John has found a new job.
約翰找到了一份新工作。

Dialogue 1

A : I cannot believe it!
我真不敢相信！

B : What's the matter?
發生了什麼問題？

A : Nothing is the matter.
John has found a new job.
He can finally leave that horrible firm.
沒事。
約翰找到了一份新工作。
他終於可以離開那間糟透了的公司。

B: That is good news.
I know he wasn't happy at his present job.
那是好消息。我知道他做現在的工作並不開心。

Dialogue 2

A : Why are you moving to New York?
你為什麼要搬去紐約？

B : John has found a new job.

The headquarters are in New York.

約翰找到了一份新工作。

總公司在紐約。

A : Well, good luck to you two.

嗯，祝你們兩個好運。

B : Thanks.　We're really going to miss everybody.

謝謝。我們真的會想念大家。

單字

found	[faʊnd]	動 找到（**find** 的過去式、過去分詞）
finally	[ˈfaɪn̩lɪ]	形 最終；終於
horrible	[ˈhɔrəbl̩]	形 （口語）糟透的
firm	[fɝm]	名 公司
present	[ˈprɛzn̩t]	形 目前的
news	[njuz]	名 新聞

UNIT 63 I've just had lunch.

我才剛吃過午飯。

Dialogue 1

A : I'm going to the deli.
Did you want something to eat?

我要去小吃店。

你想要吃什麼東西嗎？

B : No thanks, I've just had lunch.

不，謝謝，我才剛吃過午飯。

A : Brown-bagging it today huh?

今天帶便當啊？

B : Yes, my wife likes to fix my lunch.

是呀對，我太太喜歡幫我準備午餐。

Dialogue 2

A : Good morning. There are donuts and coffee if you'd like.

早安。你要來點甜甜圈和咖啡嗎？

B : Thanks, but I've just had breakfast.

謝謝，但是我才剛吃過早餐。

A : Help yourself to some coffee then.

那自己倒些咖啡吧。

B : Maybe I will, thank you.

也許我會，謝謝。

單字

fix	[fɪks]	動 準備（飯菜）
donut	[ˈdonət]	名 甜甜圈
yourself	[jʊrˈsɛlf]	代 你自己

UNIT 64 | I've already mailed it.

MP3-65

我已經寄了。

Dialogue 1

A : Do you know where that medical bill is?

你知道那個醫藥費帳單在哪嗎？

B : I've already mailed it. Why?

我已經寄了。怎麼了？

A : I just wanted to see the itemized charges.

我只是想看看各項收費。

B : Oh I've still got that.
I'll get it for you.

哦，我還有那個。
我拿給你。

Dialogue 2

A : Hey, I found another picture to put in your mother's package.

嘿，我找到另一張照片要放在你媽媽的包裹裏。

B： Oh, I've already mailed it.

噢，我已經寄出去了。

A： That's okay.

We'll just send it separately.

沒關係。

我們就把它分開寄出去。

B： That's a good idea.

那是個好主意。

單字

medical	[ˈmɛdɪkḷ]	形 醫藥的
bill	[bɪl]	名 帳單
itemized	[ˈaɪtəmˌaɪzd]	形 分項的
charge	[tʃɑrdʒ]	名 收費
separately	[ˈsɛpəˌretlɪ]	副 分開的

UNIT 65 | She has gone to Paris.

MP3-66

她去巴黎了。

Dialogue 1

A : May I speak with Mary?
我可以和瑪麗通話嗎？

B : Mary is on vacation.
She has gone to Paris.
瑪麗休假中。
她去巴黎了。

A : Oh my! Do you know when she'll be back?
哦，哎呀！你知道她什麼時候回來嗎？

B : She's due back in the office next Monday.
她應該下週一會回來上班。

Dialogue 2

A : I haven't seen Mary for a long time. Have you?

我已經很久沒見到瑪麗了。你呢？

B : Mary's on vacation.

She has gone to London for two weeks.

瑪麗休假去了。

她去倫敦二個禮拜。

A : I feel dumb. I had no idea.

我好像傻子一樣。一點也不知道。

B : Don't feel dumb.

She really didn't tell anyone until the day before her flight.

別自個兒覺得傻。

在她坐飛機走的前一天，她真的沒有告訴任何人

單字

vacation	[vəˈkeʃən]	名 假期
due	[dju]	形 到期
dumb	[dʌm]	形 愚笨的

MP3-67

UNIT 66 | I've never smoked.

我從不吸煙。

Dialogue 1

A : Care for a cigarette?

來根香煙嗎？

B : No thanks. I've never smoked.

不，謝謝。我從不吸煙。

A : Probably a good idea.
It's hard to stop once you start.

那也許是個好點子。
一旦你開始了就很難停止。

B : Well, my parents taught me that.
They both died of lung cancer.

嗯，我的爸媽有就是血淋淋的例子。
他們都因肺癌過世。

Dialogue 2

A : Do you mind if I smoke?

你介意我抽煙嗎？

B : No not at all.

You know, I've never smoked.

I just never wanted to.

不，一點也不。

你知道，我從不吸煙。

我只是從未想過要抽。

A : Are you saying that you'd like to try now?

你是說你現在想試試看？

B : Yeah, I'll try one.

是啊，我來試一根。

單字

cigarette	[sɪgəˈrɛt]	名 香煙
smoke	[smok]	動 抽煙
parent	[ˈpɛrənt]	名 雙親之一
try	[traɪ]	動 嘗試

UNIT 67

John hasn't written to me for nearly a month.

MP3-68

約翰已經幾乎一個月沒有寫信給我了。

Dialogue 1

A : Why do you look so blue, Mary?

你為什麼看來這麼憂鬱，瑪麗？

B : I'm just a little worried.

John hasn't written to me for nearly a month.

我只是有一點擔心。

約翰已經幾乎一個月沒有寫信給我了。

A : Did you try calling him?

你有試著打電話給他嗎？

B : If he is out on the battlefield, I can't call him.

I'm just going to have to wait for a letter.

如果他出外去戰場，我不能打電話給他。

我只能等待他的來信。

Dialogue 2

A : Have you heard from Sam?

你有山姆的消息嗎？

B : No, I haven't.
He hasn't written to me for nearly a month.

不，沒收到。他已經幾乎一個月沒有寫信給我了。

A : I'm sure school is keeping him very busy.

我相信確定學校課業讓他一直非常忙碌。

B : I guess so.
But I wish he would write.

我想也是。但是我希望他有來信。

單字

blue	[blu]	形 憂鬱的
worried	[ˈwɝɪd]	形 憂心；擔心
nearly	[ˈnɪrlɪ]	副 幾乎
battlefield	[ˈbætl̩fild]	名 戰場
busy	[ˈbɪzɪ]	形 忙的

UNIT 68 | I haven't seen Mary lately. 我最近沒有看到瑪麗。

MP3-69

Dialogue 1

A : What's been going on? How's Gina?

近來如何？吉娜好嗎？

B : I haven't seen Gina lately.

我最近沒有看到吉娜。

A : Why not?

I thought you two were tight.

為什麼沒有？

我以為你們兩個很親密。

B : Well, we still are I guess.

She just got a big promotion at work that keeps her busy.

嗯，我想我們仍然是。

她剛獲得大幅升遷讓她很忙。

Dialogue 2

A : It's so good to see you, Mary.

很高興見到妳，瑪麗。

B : You too.

Say, have you heard from Frank?

我也是。

嘿，有法蘭克的消息嗎？

A : You know, I haven't seen him lately.

I hear he's digging at a site in Cairo.

你知道，我最近沒見到他。

我聽說他在開羅挖掘一個地方。

B : Really? How interesting.

I've always wanted to visit Cairo.

真的？真有趣。

我一直想要去開羅參觀。

單字

lately	[ˈletlɪ]	副 近來；最近的
tight	[taɪt]	形 緊密的
promotion	[prəˈmoʃən]	名 升遷
dig	[dɪg]	動 挖掘
site	[saɪt]	名 地方

UNIT 69 | I haven't seen you in a while.

MP3-70

我有一段時間沒見到你了。

Dialogue 1

A : Hey, how are you?

I haven't seen you in a while.

嗨，你好嗎？

我有一段時間沒見到你了。

B : I haven't been feeling very well lately.

My cancer came back a couple of weeks ago.

我最近身體不是很好。

幾個禮拜前我的癌症復發了。

A : Oh, I'm so sorry to hear that.

I guess you're going through the chemo again.

噢，我很遺憾聽到這件事那個。

我想你又要經歷一次化療了。

B : Yes, unfortunately.

It worked last time.

Maybe it will work again.

是的，很不幸的。

它上次有效。

也許這一次還是會有效。

Dialogue 2

A : So how's school going?
I heard you're having some difficulties.

學校怎麼樣？
我聽說你碰到了一些困難。

B : Yeah, I haven't been doing so well lately.
My mind is on other things.

是啊，我最近表現做的不是很好。
我腦子在想其他的事。

A : Girls, right?
I was the same way at your age.

想女孩子，對嗎？
我在你這個的年紀時也和你一樣。

B : That's what dad says, too.
It still doesn't make concentrating on my schoolwork
any easier.

爸也是這麼說。
這樣說沒有讓我更能專心於課業。

單字

cancer	[ˈkænsə]	名 癌；癌症
unfortunately	[ʌnˈfɔrtʃənɪtlɪ]	副 不幸地
difficulty	[ˈdɪfəkʌltɪ]	名 困難
concentrate	[ˈkɑnsɛnˌtret]	動 集中；專心

心靈雞湯

Think big thoughts, but relish small pleasures.
深深思考人生大事，細細品嚐生活樂趣。

UNIT 70 Have you just arrived?

妳剛到嗎？

Dialogue 1

A : Margaret! Hi!
I was looking for you outside.

瑪格麗特！嗨！
我正在外面找你。

B : Hello, have you just arrived?

哈囉，妳剛到嗎？

A : Yes, just a few minutes ago.
Has the play started yet?

是的，就在幾分鐘前。
表演已經開始了嗎？

B : Oh no, not for another ten minutes.
Let's grab our seats.

哦，不，還有十分鐘才開演。
讓我們找位子坐。

Dialogue 2

A : And here is our host Mr. Green.

這是我們的主人格林先生。

B : Hello Joan, have you just arrived?

哈囉！喬安，妳剛到嗎？

A : Oh no, I've been here for almost an hour.

哦，不，我已經到了快一個小時了。

B : I'm sorry I couldn't get to you sooner.
I was putting the kids to bed.

很抱歉我沒有早點來。

我在叫小孩上床睡覺。

單字

outside	[ˈaʊtˈsaɪd]	形 外面
arrive	[əˈraɪv]	動 抵達
seat	[sit]	名 座位
host	[host]	名 主人
sooner	[ˈsunɚ]	形 早一點(soon 的比較級)

UNIT 71 | Have you ever gone skiing?

MP3-72

你曾經滑過雪嗎？

Dialogue 1

A : Have you ever gone skiing?

你曾經滑過雪嗎？

B : Oh yes, I used to go to Vale every Spring Break.

哦，是的，我每年春假都去山谷。

A : I've been trying to decide what to do on my vacation and I was thinking that skiing might be fun.

我一直在想在假期要做什麼，而我在想滑雪應該很好玩。

B : It is. You'll like it a lot.

Even when I was a beginner I had a great time.

它很好玩。你會很喜歡它。

即使我還是個初學者時，我也玩得很愉快。

Dialogue 2

A : John, have you ever heard of Donaco Systems?

約翰，你聽說過 Donaco 系統嗎？

B : I don't think so, why?

沒聽過，為何這麼問？

A : I heard that it was supposed to be a top-notch computer firm.

我聽說它被認為是頂級的電腦公司。

B : Well, if it was, I think I would have heard of it. But I'll check it out.

嗯，如果它是，我想我應該聽過。

但是我會去查一查。

單字

ski	[skɪ]	動 滑雪
decide	[dɪˈsaɪd]	動 決定
beginner	[bɪˈgɪnɚ]	名 初學者
firm	[fɝm]	名 公司

UNIT 72 | Have you heard from Tina?

你有蒂娜的消息嗎？

Dialogue 1

A : Have you heard from Tina?
I have been trying to get a hold of her all week.

你有蒂娜的消息嗎？
我一整個禮拜都在試著與她聯絡。

B : I talked to her yesterday morning.
She said that she would be working downtown all week.

我昨天早上有和她談話。
她說她整個禮拜都會在城裏工作。

A : Do you know how I could contact her down there?

你知道我要如何才能聯絡上她嗎？

B : I think I have her cell phone number here.

我想我這裏有她的手機號碼。

Dialogue 2

A : Hey, have you heard from Mary?

　　嗨，你有瑪麗的消息嗎？

B : No, why?

　　沒有，為什麼這麼問？

A : She was supposed to bring the flowers.

　　她應該會帶花過來。

B : Well, Mary is pretty reliable.
　　 I'm sure she'll be here soon.

　　嗯，瑪麗很可靠。

　　我確定她很快就來了。

單字

contact	[ˈkɑntækt]	動 聯繫
reliable	[rɪˈlaɪəbl̩]	形 可信賴的；可靠的
soon	[sun]	副 很快地

UNIT 73 Has it stopped raining yet?

MP3-74

雨停了嗎？

Dialogue 1

A : What a day. Has it stopped raining yet?

什麼鬼天氣呀。雨停了嗎？

B : Unfortunately, no.
It doesn't look like it's going to let up any time soon either.

很不幸的，沒有。
它看起來不像是很快就會停。

A : Man, I have a date tonight.
I hate wearing a raincoat to pick someone up.

老兄，我今晚有個約會。
我討厭穿著雨衣去接人。

B : So take an umbrella.

那帶把雨傘吧。

Dialogue 2

A : Has it stopped snowing yet?
I want to go play outside.
雪已經停了嗎？
我想要去外面玩。

B : Honey, it's not a good idea to play in a blizzard.
親愛的，在大風雪中去玩不是個好點子。

A : Can I make some hot cocoa then?
那我可以來一些熱可可嗎？

B : Sure. I'll go heat the milk for you.
當然。我去幫你熱牛奶。

單字

date	[det]	名 約會
raincoat	['ren,kot]	名 雨衣
umbrella	[ʌm'brɛlə]	名 雨傘
blizzard	['blɪzɚd]	名 大風雪

UNIT 74 | Have you bought a car?

MP3-75

你買了車子嗎？

Dialogue 1

A : Do you need a ride, John?

你需要搭便車嗎，約翰？

B : No thanks, I've got it covered.

不，謝謝，我有方法。

A : Have you bought a car or something?

你買了車子，還是什麼嗎？

B : Or something.
I've got a bus pass now.
I'll be using public transportation from now on.

或是什麼。
我買了公車月票。
現在起我會搭乘大眾交通工具。

Dialogue 2

A : You look different.
Have you bought a new suit?

你看起來不一樣。
你買了新衣服嗎？

B : Why, yes I have.
Do you like it?

是的，我有。你喜歡它嗎？

A : I love it.
It makes you look distinguished.

我喜歡。它讓你看起來很高貴。

B : Thanks, I thought so, too.

謝謝，我也這麼覺得。

單字

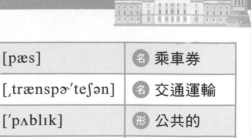

pass	[pæs]	名 乘車券
transportation	[ˌtrænspɚ'teʃən]	名 交通運輸
public	['pʌblɪk]	形 公共的
distinguished	[dɪs'tɪŋgwɪʃd]	形 出色的

MEMO

CHAPTER 8

Used to

used to ＋原型動詞，用來說明一件過去你習慣做，但是現在已經不再做的事情。

A used to 指的是過去的事情，只有過去式，沒有現在式，現在進行式或是現在完成式。

如果有人問你有在打球嗎，這句話要用「現在式」來問：
Do you play any sports?

如果你回答說，我會打網球，也是要用「現在式」來回答：
I play tennis.

但是，如果你以前常打網球，但是現在已經不打了，要說：
I used to play tennis.

B used to 的疑問句，就是用來問對方，你以前做這件事嗎？

例如：你問對方你以前在學校時有打足球嗎？英語就是：
Did you use to play football at school?

UNIT 75 | I used to play tennis a lot.

MP3-76

我以前常打網球。

Dialogue 1

A : Do you play any sports?

你有玩任何運動嗎？

B : I used to play tennis a lot, but now I'm too lazy.

我以前曾經常打網球，但是現在我太懶惰了。

A : Maybe we can play a game later this afternoon, lazy-boy.

也許我們今天下午晚點時我們可以打場球，懶惰鬼。

B : Just let me sit in the sun and relax.
I'll play tomorrow.

就讓我坐在陽光下輕鬆一下吧。
我明天和你打。

Dialogue 2

A : My fingers are killing me.
I'm learning how to sew.

我的手指痛的要命。我在學裁縫。

B : I used to sew a lot, but now I just don't have the time.

我以前常常做縫紉，但是現在我就是沒有時間。

A : What did you sew?

你縫什麼東西？

B : Everything – clothes, drapes, costumes.
　You name it, I sewed it.

什麼都有－衣服，窗簾，服裝。

你說的出來的，我都能縫。

單字

tennis	[tɛnɪs]	名	網球
sport	[sport]	名	運動
lazy	['lezɪ]	形	怠惰的
relax	[rɪ'læks]	動	放輕鬆
finger	['fɪŋgɚ]	名	手指
sew	[so]	動	縫補

UNIT 76
We used to live in a small town.

MP3-77

我們以前住在小城裏。

Dialogue 1

A : How do you like New York?

你喜歡紐約嗎？

B : We're still getting used to how big it is.
We used to live in a small town.

我們仍在習慣它的巨大。
我們以前住在小城裏。

A : What town was that?

哪一個城？

B : We lived in Nederland, Texas for twenty years before we moved to New York.

在我們搬來紐約前，我們在德州里德蘭住了二十年。

Dialogue 2

A : Do you and your wife go out much?

你和你的太太常出門嗎？

B : We used to go out all the time, but since the baby arrived, we stay in most of the time.

我們以前常出門，但是自從孩子出生後，我們大部分的時間待在家裏。

A : Well, if you'd like to go out, we can baby-sit for you.

嗯，如果你們想要出門，我們可以幫你們帶小孩。

B : That's very nice of you.
We just might do that.

你們真是非常的好心。
我們可能會那麼做。

單字

Move	[muv]	動 搬家
baby-sit	[ˈbebɪˌsɪt]	動 代看小孩
lazy	[ˈlezɪ]	形 怠惰的

UNIT 77 | Did you use to play in a band?

MP3-78

你以前有在樂團演奏過嗎？

Dialogue 1

A : Hey Tom, did you use to play in a band?
嗨，湯姆，你以前有在樂團演奏過嗎？

B : Yes, I did.
It was just a little garage band back home.
是的，我有。
那只是在家鄉時的一個小型車庫樂團。

A : Do you think you could give mc guitar lessons?
你想你可以幫我上吉他課嗎？

B : Yeah. I'd have to brush up, but I'd love to.
好啊。我需要溫習一下，但是我很樂意。

Dialogue 2

A : Did you use to live in Wisconsin?

你以前住在威斯康辛嗎？

B : No, I lived in Maryland before I moved here.

不，在搬來這裏之前，我住在馬里蘭。

A : For some reason, I was thinking that you had lived in Wisconsin.

不知為何，我以為你以前住在威斯康辛。

B : You're probably thinking of my brother.
He lived in Wisconsin for eight years.

你可能是想成我的兄弟了。

他在威斯康辛住了八年。

單字

band	[bænd]	名 樂團
garage	[gə'rɑʒ]	名 車庫
reason	['rizn̩]	名 理由

CHAPTER 9

助動詞

助動詞在學習英語是很重要的一部份，很多意思的表達需要靠助動詞才能表達的清楚。我教英語的時候，最強調的就是要學生先學會動詞的時式，和助動詞，學會了這兩部分，就好像在蓋大樓，把基石墊的很紮實。

A 當你要表示，某件事是可能的，或是某個人有能力作某件事，就要用 can。

例如：你買了新房子，你很興奮的告訴朋友說，從我家的客廳「可以」看到一個漂亮的湖，這裡的「可以」，英語就是 can。

We can see the lake from our living room window.

或者你要告訴對方，我「會」說五種語言，這裡的「會」就是表示一個人的能力，英語就是 can，

I can speak five languages.

B can 既然是表示「可以」，那你若是有事，不能來參加朋友的宴會，那就要用 can't，

例如：

I can't come to your party on Friday. 我不能參加妳星期五的宴會。

C 問對方「會」做某件事嗎，當然要用以 can 為助動詞的疑問句。

例如：問對方會游泳嗎？

Can you swim?

D 對某件事的猜測。

例如：約翰沒有來上學，你猜他「可能」是病了，你並不確定約翰是病了，你只是猜測而已，這種情形，你可以用助動詞 could，may 或 might，說：

He could be sick.

He may be sick.

He might be sick.

以上三句話，都可以用來表示你對某件事的「猜測」。

E **can't 表示「猜測」時，就是中文說的「那是不可能的」，can't 在這裡的用法，是表示「很肯定」的認為，某件事是不可能的。**

例如：約翰沒來上學，有人猜測約翰可能是病了，你說 He can't be sick. 他不可能病了，因為你前一天還跟他在一起到深夜，臨分別時他還活蹦亂跳的，精神好的很，怎麼可能一夜就病了。

F **剛剛我們說過，對某件事的猜測，英語可以用助動詞 could，may 或 might。**

例如：有人在找約翰，你猜他可能在圖書館，你可以說： He could be at the library.

He may be at the library.

或是

He might be at the library.

但是如果你「很肯定」約翰一定是在圖書館，你就要說，

He must be at the library.

UNIT 78 | You can see the lake from the window.

從窗戶看出去可以看到湖。

Dialogue 1

A : What a great house!
This is really beautiful!

這房子真棒！真漂亮！

B : Wait untill you see the living room.
You can see the lake from the window.

等你看到客廳再說吧！
從窗戶看出去可以看到湖。

A : Wow! That's gorgeous!
You did this yourself?

哇！真是太美了！
這是你自己蓋的嗎？

B : Well, I didn't actually build it, but this house is my
design – my dream house.

房子不是我蓋的，但是我設計的，這是我夢寐以求的房子。

Dialogue 2

A : The hotel doesn't look like much but all the rooms have great views.

這旅館看起來沒什麼特別之處，但每個房間都可看到很好的景觀。

B : You weren't kidding.
You can see the mountains from the balcony.

你說的是真的。
這個陽台可以看到山。

A : They're breathtaking, aren't they?

它們真的令人嘆為觀止，對吧？

B : You're telling me.
I don't think I've seen anything so beautiful.

一點也不錯。
我想以前從沒看過這麼美的景色。

心靈雞湯

lift a finger
就是舉手之勞的意思。

單字

until	[ʌnˈtɪl]	介 直到
gorgeous	[ˈgɔrdʒəs]	形 （口語）很美好的
actually	[ˈæktʃʊəlɪ]	副 實際上；事實上
build	[bɪld]	動 建造
design	[dɪˈzaɪn]	名 設計
dream	[drim]	名 夢；理想
view	[vju]	名 景觀；風景
balcony	[ˈbælkənɪ]	名 陽台
breathtaking	[ˈbrɛθtekɪŋ]	形 令人嘆為觀止的

UNIT 79

I can't come to your party on Friday.

MP3-80

我不能參加妳星期五的宴會

Dialogue 1

A : What's up, Susan?

蘇珊，有什麼事嗎？

B : Jill, I'm afraid I can't come to your party on Friday.

吉兒，我恐怕不能參加妳星期五的宴會了。

A : Why not?

為什麼？

B : I told my daughter I would go to her soccer game and then take her out to dinner.

我告訴我女兒會去看她踢足球，之後再帶她去吃晚餐。

Dialogue 2

A : Mary, I hate to do this to you, but something has come up.
I'm afraid I can't come to your party on Friday.

瑪莉，我真的不是故意的，但我臨時有事。
我恐怕不能參加妳星期五的宴會。

B : Are you kidding?
I told everyone you'd be there.

你在開玩笑吧？
我已經告訴大家你會來。

A : I know, I know. I'm sorry.
But my boss wants me to host his party for some executives.
I can't tell him no when I'm looking for promotion,

我知道，很抱歉。
但我的老闆要我幫他主辦個宴會，招待一些高級主管。
在我希望升遷的情況下，我不可能拒絕他的。

B : I guess not.
Look, try to drop by before or after you're done, okay?
Everybody wants to see you.

我想也是。
聽著，盡量試試看，在宴會開始前，或宴會後，過來看一下，好嗎？
大家都想看看你。

單字

afraid	[əˈfred]	形 恐怕
soccer	[ˈsɑkɚ]	名 足球
executive	[ɪgˈzɛkjʊtɪv]	名 主管
host	[host]	動（作主人）接待
promotion	[prəˈmoʃən]	名 升遷
boss	[bɔs]	名 主管；老闆

UNIT 80 Can you swim?

你會游泳嗎？

Dialogue 1

A : Can you swim?
你會游泳嗎？

B : Oh yes, I learned how to swim when I was little.
我會，小時候就學會游泳了。

A : Would you like to go to the beach with me then?
那你想和我一起去海邊嗎？

B : I'd love to.
It's been a long time since I've been to the beach.
好啊。
我好久沒有去海邊了。

Dialogue 2

A : Hey, John, can you set up this stereo system?
嗨，約翰，你會不會組裝這個音響？

B : I can if there are instructions.

　　如果有組裝說明書，應該沒問題。

....

A : I've got the instructions right here.

　　我這裡有說明書。

....

B : Okay, then. Could you bring me my toolbox?

　　好的，你可不可以幫我把工具箱拿過來？

....

單字

swim	[swɪm]	動	游泳
learn	[lɝn]	動	學習
beach	[bitʃ]	名	海濱
since	[sɪns]	副	自從
stereo	[ˈstɛrɪˌo]	名	立體音響
system	[ˈsɪstəm]	名	系統
instructions	[ɪnˈstrʌkʃənz]	名	說明書

UNIT 81
He could be sick.

他可能是病了。

Dialogue 1

A : What's the matter with John?

約翰怎麼了？

B : He is looking a bit pale, isn't he?
He could be sick.

他看起來有點蒼白，對不對？
可能是生病了。

A : Why doesn't he go home?

那他為什麼不回家呢？

B : He's a workhorse.
He'll keep at his work until he drops.

他是勞碌命。
要忙到倒下來才會停。

Dialogue 2

A : Is Mary all right?
She's been acting odd lately.

> 瑪麗還好吧？
> 她最近的行為舉止很怪。

B : She could be lonely.
Her boyfriend just moved away.

> 可能是寂寞吧。
> 她男朋友剛剛搬走了。

A : Oh, I didn't know.
Maybe we should invite her for dinner.

> 我不知道這回事。
> 也許我們可以邀請她一起吃晚餐。

B : That's a good idea.
Let's go ask her now.

> 這主意不錯，現在就去問她吧。

單字

pale	[pel]	形 蒼白
workhorse	[ˈwɝkhɔrs]	名 吃苦耐勞的人
drop	[drɑp]	動 倒下
odd	[ɑd]	形 奇怪的
lonely	[ˈlonlɪ]	形 寂寞的；孤獨的

MEMO

UNIT 82 | He may be at the library.

MP3-83

他可能在圖書館。

Dialogue 1

A : Do you have any idea where John is?
你知道約翰在哪裡嗎？

B : I know he had some studying to do.
He may be at the library.
我知道他要唸書。
可能在圖書館吧。

A : I don't want to bother him if he's studying.
如果他在讀書的話，我不想吵他。

B : He should be back soon.
You can wait here for him if you like.
他應該快回來了。
如果願意的話，你可以在這裡等他。

Dialogue 2

A : Does anyone know what happened to Mary?
有沒有人知道瑪麗怎麼了？

B : She may be stuck in traffic.

I just heard on the radio that highway 90 is backed up.

她可能碰上交通堵塞了。

我剛剛在收音機上聽到，90 號公路交通堵住了。

A : Great. Okay, who can cover for Mary if she doesn't make it on time?

好的，如果她不能準時到，有沒有人可以負責她的部分？

B : I guess I can.

我想我可以。

單字

library	[ˈlaɪˌbrɛrɪ]	名 圖書館
bother	[ˈbɑðɚ]	動 打擾
back	[bæk]	動 回來
traffic	[ˈtræfɪk]	名 交通

MP3-84

UNIT 83 It may be my mother.

可能是我媽。

Dialogue 1

A : Could you answer the phone?
It may be my mother.
你能不能接個電話？
可能是我媽打來的。

B : It was a wrong number.
Why did you expect your mother?
是打錯電話的。
你為什麼會覺得是你媽打來的？

A : She was going to call after she got out of surgery.
她手術結束後，會打電話過來。

B : I'd like to talk to her when she calls.
她打電話來時，我想和她說話。

Dialogue 2

A : Who's at the door?
誰在門口？

B ： It may be another salesman.

可能是另一個銷售員。

A ： Well, don't answer then.
I'd rather pretend we weren't home.

那就不要應門。

我寧可假裝我們都不在家。

B ： I know. It seems like the only people who come to our house anymore are salesmen.

我知道，好像只有銷售員會來我們家。

單字

wrong	[rɔŋ]	形 錯誤的
expect	[ɪk'spɛkt]	動 期待
surgery	['sɝdʒərɪ]	名 手術
salesman	['selzmən]	名 推銷員
pretend	[prɪ'tɛnd]	動 假裝

UNIT 84 | She may not be at home.

MP3-85

她有可能不在家。

Dialogue 1

A : Do you know how to get a hold of Mary?

你知道怎樣聯絡上瑪麗嗎？

B : I have her home phone number, but she may not be at home.

我有她家裡的電話號碼，但她有可能不在家。

A : Well, give it to me anyway.
I have to try and reach her.

不妨把號碼給我吧。

我得試著聯絡她。

B : Okay. It's 343-2156.

好的，她的電話是 343-2156。

Dialogue 2

A： Why won't Frank sign the agreement?

法蘭克為什麼不簽那份合約呢？

B： He may not want to put anything down on paper yet.

他也許還不想立下白紙黑字吧。

A： But he came in asking us to buy his property.

但他來拜訪我們，希望我們買下他的房地產。

B： It doesn't make sense to me either, but what can we do?

我也不懂啊，但我們又能怎麼做呢？

單字

reach	[ritʃ]	動 聯絡上
agreement	[əˈgrimənt]	名 同意書
sign	[saɪn]	動 簽名
property	[ˈprɑpɚtɪ]	名 地產

UNIT 85 | She may not be able to find our house. 她可能找不到我們的家。

MP3-86

Dialogue 1

A : Joan is not too good with directions.
She may not be able to find our house.

瓊安不是很有方向感。
她可能找不到我們的家。

B : She does have a map.
I'm sure she'll be fine.

她有地圖。
我想她沒問題的。

A : I know. I just worry.
I'd hate for her to get lost.

我知道，我只是擔心。
真的不希望她迷路。

B : She has our number in case anything happens.

如果有事情發生的話，她有我們的電話號碼。

Dialogue 2

A : Greg called.
He said he may not be able to come to the party.

格瑞打電話過來。
他說可能沒辦法來參加舞會了。

B : Why?

為什麼？

A : His daughter is having problems.
He wants to make sure she's okay.

他女兒有一些問題。
他要確定她沒問題。

B : He definitely is a devoted father.

他真是個好父親。

單字

directions	[dəˈrɛkʃənz]	名 方向指示
map	[mæp]	名 地圖
problem	[ˈprɑbləm]	名 問題
definitely	[ˈdɛfənətlɪ]	副 確定地；肯定地
devoted	[dɪˈvotɪd]	形 摯愛的

UNIT 86 | He may not like this movie.
MP3-87

他可能不喜歡這部電影。

Dialogue 1

A : I don't know if an action flick is James's cup of tea.
我不知道詹姆士喜不喜歡看動作片？

B : You're right. He may not like this movie.
你顧慮的對，他可能不喜歡這部電影。

A : What about a drama?
He might like that.
那劇情片如何？
他可能會喜歡那個。

B : Yeah, let's get a drama.
好吧，就找部劇情片吧。

Dialogue 2

A : I thought John was a vegetarian.
He may not enjoy a steak dinner.

我認為約翰吃素。
他可能不會喜歡吃牛排大餐。

B : Oh, you're right.
We'll find a good vegetarian restaurant.

你說的沒錯。
那找一家不錯的素食餐廳吧。

A : I hope you know of some because I don't.

希望你知道一些素食餐廳，因為我對這個一點也不知道。

B : We'll call Margaret.
She'd know a good place.

我們可以打電話給瑪格麗特。
她會知道哪家素食餐廳好。

單字

action	[ˈækʃən]	名 動作
flick	[flɪk]	名（口語）電影
drama	[ˈdrɑmə]	名 戲劇
vegetarian	[ˌvɛdʒəˈtɛrɪən]	名 素食者
steak	[stek]	名 牛排
restaurant	[ˈrɛstərənt]	名 餐館；飯店

MEMO

UNIT 87 It can't be true.

MP3-88

這不可能的。

Dialogue 1

A : Did you hear that they're firing Jack?

你有聽說他們要炒傑克魷魚嗎？

B : What? It can't be true.

Where did you hear that?

什麼，這不可能的。

你從哪裡聽說的？

A : From the head guy himself.

Apparently, his performance has dropped steadily.

從老闆那裡聽到的。

很明顯的，他最近的表現一直不佳。

B : That's not fair.

They are the ones who overloaded him.

這真是太不公平了。

是他們把這麼多工作堆到他身上，才會這樣子的。

Dialogue 2

A : Mary and John are getting married?
It can't be true.
They fight all the time.

瑪麗和約翰要結婚了？
這是不可能的。
他們一天到晚都在吵架。

B : Well, it's true.
Here's the invitation to prove it.

這是真的。
這份邀請卡就是證明。

A : That is so weird.
 I ought to buy them a punching bag for a wedding present.

那真是怪了。
我應該買一個沙袋送給他們當作結婚禮物。

B : That would not be very romantic.

那就太不羅曼蒂克了。

單字

fire	[faɪr]	動 解雇
performance	[pɚˈfɔrməns]	名 表現
drop	[drɑp]	動 下降
fair	[fɛr]	形 公平的
invitation	[ɪnvɪˈteʃən]	名 邀請卡
weird	[wɪrd]	形 奇怪的

MEMO

UNIT 88　You can't be serious.

MP3-89

你不是說真的吧。

Dialogue 1

A ： I wish we could just leave this town.

Hey! Let's fly to Mexico tonight!

我真希望我們可以離開這個小鎮。

這樣吧，我們今晚就飛去墨西哥吧。

B ： You can't be serious.

We have to work tomorrow.

你不是說真的吧。

我們明天都要上班。

A ： Call in sick.

I need a vacation, an adventure.

打電話請病假吧。

我需要休假和冒險。

B ： You need to go to bed so you can go to work tomorrow.

你需要早點上床，這樣明天才能上班。

Dialogue 2

A : What if we dressed up as a horse for Halloween?

萬聖節時，我們打扮成一匹馬，好不好？

B : You can't be serious.

That would be torture to be in the same costume.

你不是說真的吧。

兩個人在同一套衣服裡，這很折磨人呢。

A : Come on. No one else will do that.

We'll be original.

拜託嘛，沒有人會這麼做。

我們會是第一個這樣做的人。

B : Only if you are the back end of the horse.

只要你做馬尾，我就同意。

單字

serious	[ˈsɪrɪəs]	形 認真的
adventure	[ədˈvɛntʃɚ]	名 冒險；冒險片
torture	[ˈtɔrtʃɚ]	名 折磨

UNIT 89

He must be at the library. 他一定是在圖書館。

MP3-90

Dialogue 1

A : I have called everywhere looking for John.
我打電話到每個地方在找約翰。

B : He must be at the library.
He has a paper to write.
他一定在圖書館。
他有個報告要寫。

A : Well, I'm on my way home.
I guess I could stop by there.
我現在要回家了。
我想路上我可以順道去一下圖書館。

B : If you find him, tell him thanks for lunch.
如果你找到他，幫我謝謝他請我吃午餐這件事。

Dialogue 2

A : Do you know where Mary is?
你知道瑪麗在哪裡嗎？

B : If she's not at her house, she must be at her boyfriend's.

如果她不在家，就一定在她男朋友那裡。

A : I don't want to call over there.
I'll talk to her some other time.

我不想打電話到那裡去。

另外再找時間和她談話好了。

B : She'll probably leave his house soon.
Just keep trying her at home.

她可能很快就會離開她男朋友家。

繼續撥她家裡的電話吧。

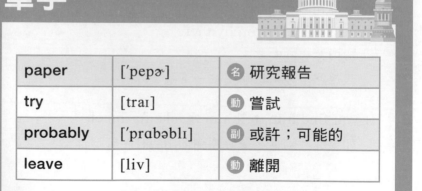

單字

paper	[ˈpepɚ]	名 研究報告
try	[traɪ]	動 嘗試
probably	[ˈprɑbəblɪ]	副 或許；可能的
leave	[liv]	動 離開

MP3-91

UNIT 90 You must be Mary.

妳一定是瑪麗吧。

Dialogue 1

A : You must be Mary.
Lisa has told me so much about you.
妳一定是瑪麗吧。
麗莎告訴我好多有關妳的事。

B : Yes, I am. It's nice to meet you.
我是，很高興認識妳。

A : Likewise. Can I get you anything?
我也是，妳要不要喝點什麼？

B : A drink would be nice.
飲料就可以了。

Dialogue 2

A ： Miss Lee, here is your package.

李小姐，妳的包裹。

B ： You must be mistaken.

I'm not expecting a package.

你一定是弄錯了。

我並沒有在等包裹。

A ： Are you Sandra Lee?

妳是珊德拉李嗎？

B ： No, I'm Mary.

Sandra is on the third floor.

不，我是瑪麗，珊德拉住三樓。

單字

package	[ˈpækɪdʒ]]	名 包裹
mistaken	[məˈstekən]	形 弄錯了
expect	[ɪkˈspɛkt]	動 預期；期待

Live simply.
生活簡單。
Think quickly.

思考敏捷。
Work diligently.
工作勤奮。

MEMO

MEMO

Use less salt，eat less red meat.
少用鹽巴，少吃紅肉。

MEMO

MEMO

英文裡，私奔叫做 elope。 聽起來是不是很像閩南話的「伊落跑」
呢？

MEMO

MEMO

Think big thoughts, but relish small pleasures.
深深思考人生大事，細細品嚐生活樂趣。

MEMO

國家圖書館出版品預行編目資料

世界最強英文文法會話 / 蘇盈盈著
-- 新北市：哈福企業，2021.4
面；公分 . -- （英語系列；70）
ISBN 978-986-06114-1-0（平裝附 MP3）
1. 英語 2. 語法 3. 會話
805.16   110004496

英語系列：70

書名／世界最強英文文法會話
作者／蘇盈盈
出版單位／哈福企業有限公司
責任編輯／Jocelyn Chang
封面設計／八十文創
內文排版／八十文創
出版者／哈福企業有限公司
地址／新北市板橋區五權街 16 號 1 樓
電話／(02) 2808-4587 傳真／(02) 2808-6545
郵政劃撥／31598840 戶名／哈福企業有限公司
出版日期／2021 年 4 月
定價／NT$ 330 元（附 MP3）
港幣定價／110 元（附 MP3）

全球華文國際市場總代理／采舍國際有限公司
地址／新北市中和區中山路 2 段 366 巷 10 號 3 樓
電話／(02) 8245-8786 傳真／(02) 8245-8718
網址／www.silkbook.com 新絲路華文網

香港澳門總經銷／和平圖書有限公司
地址／香港柴灣嘉業街 12 號百樂門大廈 17 樓
電話／(852) 2804-6687 傳真／(852) 2804-6409

email／welike8686@Gmail.com
網址／Haa-net.com
facebook／Haa-net 哈福網路商城

Original Copyright © 3S Culture Co., Ltd.